CW00341941

Space for Farming

Pammy Riggs

Space for Farming

Pammy Riggs

Copyright © 2020

All rights reserved. No part of this publication may be reproduced, stored in a retrieval system or transmitted in any form or by any means electronic, mechanical, audio, visual or otherwise, without prior permission of the copyright owner. Nor can it be circulated in any form of binding or cover other than that in which it is published and without similar conditions including this condition being imposed on the subsequent purchaser.

ISBN: 978-1-9163876-0-7

Published by Pammy Riggs Publishing in conjunction with Writersworld. This book is produced entirely in the UK, is available to order from most book shops in the United Kingdom, and is globally available via UK-based Internet book retailers and www.amazon.com.

Copy edited by Ian Large

Cover design by Jag Lall

www.writersworld.co.uk

WRITERSWORLD
2 Bear Close Flats
Bear Close
Woodstock
Oxfordshire
OX20 1JX
United Kingdom

☎ 01993 812500

☎ +44 1993 812500

The text pages of this book are produced via an independent certification process that ensures the trees from which the paper is produced come from well managed sources that exclude the risk of using illegally logged timber while leaving options to use post-consumer recycled paper as well.

With my son, Todd, held firmly in mind.

Acknowledgements

To my most honest and open minded mentor and physics guru, Sir Oliver Lodge, who helped me through my time in Exeter University's Physics Department, and for proving our infinite interconnectedness.

Also to my son, Todd 'Iceman' Riggs, 1984-2017, whose intense and happy love for farming, the countryside, gritty farmers and most especially his dear cows, informs this plea for a rescaling of our whole food industry where, at present, the machinery is too large for the roads and the heartbreak too large for our human hearts.

Farmings' casualties are NOT fiction. This book, scoured from my heart, fits the category of 'faction'.

Chapter 1

*The scales we deal with, large and small,
have further meaning for us all.*

Dear readers, come with me on a journey of discovery – we have two very different lives to consider. One you will all be familiar with, a human, a man, his feelings and fortunes in a difficult profession where so many factors are pushing and pulling at his sensibilities. I hope you can feel along with Peter, our main man of the story but equally there is another portion of life to be considered, one entwined with our man on so many different levels. Here a tiny atom of substance, without which none of our story would exist, comes into being and pushes the fortunes of this man along, but consider for a moment. Is this tiny substance also allowed the dignity of a life? Can we also follow the entwining process close up – be there for both these beings? One a single tiny part of another's life? We shall see.

It starts here deep in the hold of a ship, a mighty vessel chundering its way from a far off land to deliver goods into a port, which port matters not. This is an everyday occurrence in our busy world.

Yes, tiny things in the hold of this mighty vessel begin to grow. The vibration of the ship gave energy and heat to a nanoparticle and, like the primal stuff of the beginnings of Life, it took that as a signal to multiply. Warmth, humidity and the deliciousness of the material it lay upon, plus the time taken on a journey of many months allowed this small beginning to flower, grow, set seeds and by the time the landing was scheduled this part of the hold was alive with the tiny, tiny spores of a new beginning. A new substance given its chance in the laboratory of life on that epic journey.

Tiny, tiny substance, just a couple of atoms wide, like an island of itself, prepared to shed one atom at a time, and multiply again and again.

Many atoms make a goo in this instance, but one is a tiny offering on its own – let us assign a meaningful life to this tiny part of the whole and follow its fortunes while the greater part has its own agenda spreading as a fungus or infection or virus might. We shall meet that portion later, time and time again.

Our tiny fellow, for it may as well be a comfortable relationship from the beginning, is a whirligig of energy, a sweeping ball surrounded on all sides by fellow atoms, each holding the other in space, their own space, pushing at each other's walls, outer perimeter to outer perimeter, jostling to take up their allotted space but never encroaching upon each other's until at some given moment when forces from one balance exactly the needs of the other they pop seamlessly into a combined existence, so happy to combine to become a couple, to change their outer form and dance together, to split and come together in a beautifully choreographed extravaganza of multiplication. Happy! happy! happy! in their lives. The inner world of our tiny atom, somehow, using the lever of desire for life, growth, multiplication, and to make its presence felt in the human scale world also.

Time to introduce our man Peter to the story. A kind, gentle man of average proportions, hard of leg, physically strong. His workout is not the falseness of the gym but good considered hard work. His legs walk him miles on hard and squishy ground, he climbs gates and steps and ladders regularly. He makes and mends, and common sense prevails in his down to earth world. Peter is a farmer, has been along that trajectory from his youth. His playground was the farm, the fields, the hay and straw bales and his great love, the animals. This strong man is gentle too. His big plates of hands, hard and leathery from many hours of 'doing'. Big do-ey hands. A handshake from Peter is like a grounding tool; his strength comes from feet firmly on the ground. Feet and hands and heart that understand the ground for what it is, our sacred ground, our food source, where we balance ourselves and take, and must also give back. He stands firmly as a guardian to this particular cycle of life. Peter the farmer, supplying your food, your sustenance whoever you are, wherever you hang your hat, our Peter gives his life to keep you in your job. Eat well.

Let us now shift attention to the tiny atom that makes up this outer world. The world you and I exist in comes into being for us to experience because of our other friend. He and his myriad friends make up your waking world's surface, the air you breathe and the food you eat. Surely due attention to such an important substance is allowed?

Is it fair to say that this little life of lives is washed along by circumstance only? Would the object in the hold of the ship have been able to jump into a multiple existence without those perfect surrounding conditions cocooning him and encouraging him? Is it to be the same for our main man, Peter; shall his existence similarly be dictated by circumstance, by the fortunes of others pushing upon his life, forcing him to make 'his' decisions along their lines? We shall find that out over the course of this story – stick with it, there are surprises to come.

Here in this world, a buzzing harmony exists for any who have the sensitivity to achieve connection. It is aligned with the feeling when standing in front of the work of a great master in a huge art gallery. Partly the awe of the surroundings, the grand stature and scale of some of the works of art give gravitas to the image portrayed but this same buzzing sentiment and feeling of true art comes from the humblest of paintings too.

Parent, think with what pride your toddler hands over the picture and explains the sky, the sun, the mum and dad and sister, described there with circular representations; string arms, legs and hair. What pride as the interpretation is reeled out from the young artist's mind and the heart swell of pride assigns itself to this grid of admiration and growing sense of learning. Take these scales: old master recognised through centuries and lauded, perhaps sold for millions; and this, the grubby, water-splashed first picture proudly presented. There may be a sibling who has helped, sensing the achievement, equally pleased to see the onward development of brother or sister. What a wonder is art, that it can fire up the surrounding grid, make a field of pride, and then build on it. Dad arrives and adds his admiration, grandparent appears and joins in. Where is all this energy coming from and going to? A place on the fridge assigned, white appliance artwork, proud glances with every walk-by, akin to the grand stature of the art gallery. Admiration piled upon admiration, art boffins stand as if in a trance, transfixed by the artistry of brushwork, of composition, of representation, figurative or abstract and above all the hidden messages so often laid out in allegory, myth-like metaphorical statements there for all to enjoy. If they are able.

Let me take you back to the atom of substance, the one that now supports you as you sit or stand upon this earth – for no doubt you do – and explain its artistry just a little. What at first seems solid is not, just as what you experience on that flat canvas surface as depiction of rose, or vase or battle scene or tiny pointillism of dots to dupe the eye into a scene, is not. Neither is this world you stand or sit upon. It supports you only because you are made of this self-same stuff, if you were tinier you would fall through its grid, like sifted flour dropping through the holes in a sieve.

Allow the smallest parts of yourself to do just that, the finest parts of you, your feelings, the ones you experience as pride, that other side of you, your soft side, pulled along by ambition, love, reason; where is that side residing? Allow that side of you – it has no scale, it cannot be said to be stuck by a gap too small to fall through, for you are the shape shifter, will yourself thinner and fall through. You need not scrape yourself on the sides of your imaginary sieve, for you can construct them of a gentle material, let the sides caress you as you travel through. They can brush away any immediate worries and cares and be, here fallen through the gap and into another world. The one where the Real You exists and makes the decisions of your life. Here the grid of solidity is gone and the world is larger than before, expansive, as huge as your imagination makes it. Or, as tiny as you will to go. This world is yours to play in, and, as the artist pulled through his ideas and laid them with skill upon the canvas to convey, and the child just learning also pulled through his idea of sun and sky and face and limb, so you have that ability too. This is where this story desires to take you. Come too, follow the thread, the one that you can, as we weave and concoct a story from something much finer than thin air, but we cannot as yet say what it is we weave it from. Your atoms support you in this place, undeniably you have knowledge of yourself existing, propped upon this strong world, but if you look close, scrutinise, they will let you through to that Other Place, and you can enjoy it too.

Look inside our tiny fellow, what do you see? Come close with the magnifying glass of imagination and knowledge. It should show us the hard inner balls of electrical substance, items strong enough to fling off whatever the firing range of our scientists can muster. Forces we hardly dare measure and cannot see but no, that is not our revelation. Something quite incredible takes place in here. The atom reveals yet tinier structures, neatly placed relevant to each other and streaming in giant – relatively speaking – whorls, snatching up an energy and mixing and matching it though a spiralling system of counter loops and rebalances. Move closer, peer deeper, the sight through this magnifier takes the breath away, ordinary vision halts and another sense takes over, one where matching the illusion of the atom is a natural move. There is still sensation, effort to make and intelligent thought in the experience of looking, none of this is removed. Time is gone, another world opens up where a life has purpose and meaning within its own sphere of understanding. Soon, we shall enter the world of animal sensibilities and be quite at home there too, transfer that same belief to this small but relevant part of the existential world and I have you with me. Good. Is it physical? Is it from a feeling world? Is it from a thinking world? We cannot know but that we test this out. First, however, there is a chap waiting for our attention and he wakes. We only observe him, do not affect him or push him or boss him – or do we?

Peter pushes back the covers in an automatic move, gestures wildly in the direction of the noise that woke him and is already half dressed before his consciousness has caught up with him. He goes to milk the cows, a warmish coffee, easier to drink than hot, in one hand, his farmer's clothing under a boiler suit and special milking wellingtons are his garb for this start to his day. The cows know and understand the routine as well as he, and file up to empty the strain on their huge distended udders. Peter gently cajoles the slow ones along, running a familiar hand down legs and backs. The rhythmic swoosh, swoosh of the machinery a usual backdrop to the morning routine. One that can never be broken. Our chap must every day, within the hour, come to the rescue of the animals or his life and theirs would be in disorder. No lie in, or Sunday off, each holiday day the same. Farming.

A crisis was upon the government with this new problem growing in the food industry. What were they to do about it? The solution had to be a practical one and one that would reach a conclusion in as short a time as possible. There was no cause for alarm. As far as they were concerned, telling the food industry to close its doors to unnecessary incoming loads was an easy solution but not so for anyone involved with the practical issues and day to day running of a business.

This threat to the food industry had first been noticed in some flour related products. It had been quite easy to stop in its tracks with applications of heat; hence no cooked foods were affected and it was soon discovered that raising temperatures by a small amount cured the problem of growth. Things became more complicated with uncooked feedstuffs and farming would be hit most.

Animal feed is delivered as a raw product, often blown into large hoppers or travelled in bags, large and small. Some bags suitable for carrying by a person and others to be hauled about on the forks of a tractor or other machine, but still raw, and often dusty and here is where the problem lay, with dust, not easily controlled. It seemed this fungus-like growth 'ate' the dust associated with grains and produced an unfamiliar taint to the feed, stimulating complaints from farmers to their suppliers, hence the panic moved up the food chain and government animal health, nutritionists and vets got involved. All applied their own knowledge and sent samples to labs to be tested. The biggest relief was that, although unsightly, there were no toxins associated with this new creature in our midst and that mild heat treatment or disinfectant killed it off smartly.

So far so good, but farmers have to feed their animals and that feed is hauled around the countryside on lorries so a countrywide disinfectant rule was put in place.

Chapter 2

*Peter aches with grief and pain; he chose this life
but feels its harshness cause him strife.*

In the morning, before 'the incident', Peter had been thinking about his plight and how to address things. For instance, if he were to stop what he was doing, there were all the back payments to take into consideration. He really wanted to keep up with all his financial commitments but when the priority *had* to be feed for the animals then there really was no choice.

Peter had already been up for hours; he had done the morning routine without thinking. It was a comfort to him to have finished that job and now he had his list, a mental list of priorities to get him safely through the day and back round in a circle to begin the milking routine again.

There was a time when he had help and that meant he could afford to stay out on the away fields long enough to complete a job. Recently he had been forced into giving up the help. After all, workers need real pay these days and what with the squeeze on the milk price again in one year, feed prices due to rise again – something to do with a tussle between oil prices in one part of the world and an over dry harvest in another, it was out of his hands. No luxuries, no more helpers which was more than a shame. He was lonely. Bringing news from off the farm was part of the fun of having help. Yes he has the radio, television and if he made the effort he could join in with all that modern stuff. But the company he craved was the camaraderie of another human being just to chat with, maybe crack the odd joke or to talk through a problem or idea. Oh well, another thing that used to be a normality had become a luxury. He sighed a long sigh.

Slightly stooped and looking older than his forty something years, he trudged off to attend to his next most important task, glancing resignedly at the dingy mess of old buckets and plastic feed sacks he had been meaning to tidy up for the past couple of weeks. When would he get to that job he wondered? Hopefully before they became invisible to him. Certainly the yard was no longer as tidy as it used to be. That was one of the things he loved, to complete a task and tidy up the tools. It so annoyed him to live with mess; he liked order in his life. Order helped him think and kept the uneasy feelings in check. He thought again about getting some help, just to carry out a few of the routine jobs and let him get to those extra things – but no way could he afford it this month, so he gave up on that and plodded on.

With a heavy heart, our man Peter took his implement and dug and dug and dug. Relentlessly he struck the ground with the spade, striking over and over again, loosening the dry shaley soil. He should have stopped and gone to get a better tool, but rage and fear and grief was upon him. How can it be that he is forced into this corner? How can it be that a little life strained for by a mother can be considered so worthless that he was to take a pistol and shoot at close range a small creature totally innocent, still struggling for breath and then he was required to pay for the removal of what was now considered a worthless carcass. Well, no longer could he bear that pain, no one ever talked about this bit of his farming life. What was there to say? The scars on his heart were invisible to those who used the milk from that cow. What about her heart, were there scars there? A mother losing a child. Why, why, why must it be this way? He had looked into her eyes, silent apology formed on his lips, these dear creatures were the ones he lived out his daily life with, they were his friends – more than the lads in the pub anyway. There he only chatted, bantered, skimmed the surface of emotion. Heard them all complain, blame each other and untouchable bodies like 'the government'. In the end he had stopped going.

Here at home it was different. Life existed at a deeper level. Mostly wordless but nevertheless deep with communication. Here you felt the conversation rather than speaking it. In this manner there were no lies, no excuses, no beating about the bush. If the channels were open then it was in rushes of emotion that communication came, in wordless but well-formed sentiment. Who could say that these dear animals, domesticated by mankind, supposedly for mutual benefit, do not have deep emotion and understanding, who? If it took thousands of years to get to this point where breeding successive generations had managed to increase the milk quotient many fold, where was the mutual benefit there? Cows now had to contend with udders so huge and distended that they forced their hind legs apart, forced them to walk unnaturally and, on the few occasions when the sun was on their back and they should feel the joy of spring in the air, even a small skip for joy and the sheer love of life would rack them with the pain of inertia, swinging udder clashing onto bony hocks and stop that small pleasure in their life. Short life, cows now had little chance of growing up properly, a decade old was a rare cow indeed. Maybe four or five lactations, and that also meant four or five calves being ripped away from her. If she was 'lucky' she was not a best milker, maybe she had been allowed to run with the bull, a natural service when she was exactly ready, when he knew and she knew, perhaps a showing of affection pre service, rare in a milk herd. At least then, Peter thought, he would not have the ultimate pain of shooting a calf, there would be a point, from the human economic view of farming to keeping this calf alive. In that case Peter could have his short time doing his level best to replace the love of that mother. Not perfect he knew, but better than this alternative.

This last calf, a perfect little bull calf for its sins, what sins? Innocence was written all over the beautiful little body lying before him, the sheen of birth not yet faded from the coat, only the dead look in the eye and the contorted unnatural position after being dumped here on the dry dusty ground next to the beginnings of a hole being dug by Peter, our man, tired, ashamed at his species giving him this job in the name of economics. Here was Peter acting out illegally, too worried about costs to disobey the 'logic' of killing male calves at birth, but willing to disobey the legalities around it by hiding this carcass in the ground, rather than pay to have it removed. It was an Indian summer, hot, and the flies were about. Leaving this calf for even half a day would cause even more pain to him. In no time bluebottles would be upon it, laying neat rows of cream coloured eggs around the eyes, the mouth, the anus. All entry points to this little body would be ingressed and probably before the warmth of calf-life was yet gone. Another life, fly-life, no lesser in its desire to procreate, making good its right to living, as any other one of God's creatures.

It was ironic that the calf under man's intervention had been born and then killed but the maggot undisturbed by man was to get the benefit, but not if Peter could help it. He struck the ground and felt the vibration of the ringing sound of steel on stone turn to sharp pain in his wrist and he sang out with an unearthly sound, part release of physical pain but more of emotional pain from this ghastly job he must do. Sense, at least in a practical way, returned to him, Peter was not a hot-headed man. He realised hurting himself would not help so he put down the spade, picked up his shovel and scooped out the loosened earth and debris. The hole had to be made here away from any water courses so the digging was hard. Small comfort that this calf would be buried on the farm where it was conceived, bad luck that his best milker, Number 476, was the mother.

She was served by artificial insemination; he had chosen her partner hoping against hope that she would produce a heifer calf to add to his special line. His best milker, Number 476, was not the sort of 'best' that most farmers would consider. She was a small cow by standards of the breed, not the most prolific milker but his best, in the sense that she gave him the most joy. He had put her to a milk bull; by rights she should have had semen from a meat animal, if he had done that then he would not now be burying this calf – male or female it would most likely have survived another couple of years but not on his farm. He had to give up his calves. His plan, his plot, was to introduce into his herd those cattle who 'spoke' to him. If Number 476 had borne a heifer, a female calf, he could in all conscience have kept her for a replacement milker and she would have been soon reunited with her mum in the herd. What he wanted most of all were happy animals and as clear a conscience as he could muster in these harsh days of farming. If he could do anything to alleviate his pain at hurting his girls that is what he was doing. Defying logic, he had put this cow to a milk bull and it had all backfired in his face, leaving him the worst of alternatives, a dead calf to deal with, more guilt to tuck away into his overloaded soul and his favourite cow to face at next milking. He would be able to tell she was grieving. Not just from the pained lowing that would go on into the night but she would be restless, searching in each corner of the barn. She would stay in for a day or two, just to check all the mechanics of birth had progressed; parturition, followed by colostrum and a cleansing, the large placenta had to loosen and remove itself. Once these events had passed the cow could return to the herd, to the pasture and hopefully to some comfort in her crowd. They all knew the pain of separation, the milkers, our brave girls.

Peter completed his unwanted task, his illegal task. At least he would not have the guilt-reminding stench of a fast rotting carcass to contend with. He could not afford a visit from the renderers for every dead calf and stockpiling was out of the question at this time of year.

He went back to the mother, she stood with head low. Fighting his desire to leave this job, find another less heart-rending place to be on the farm, he approached her, a low noise emitted from his throat, visceral, ancient, creeping through his body, a kind of thrill of desperation. He was back, somewhere else in his physical body had opened up, the touch of his hand on this cow's back, the solid feel of her fur, short coat, and skin covering a bony frame, this touch went deeper than ever before he had felt. 'I'm sorry old girl, I tried to keep her with you, I tried but I can't make it happen.' He leant over her, joined in hopelessness with this mother, childless again and not for want of trying. His throat tight, aching, tearless, nevertheless crying inside.

Her body had eagerly accepted sperm from any source that would stick. She had felt and enjoyed the cow child within her, made loving moans towards it in the womb. She knew she was being prepared by evolution for motherhood, her senses being heightened to accept, love and protect this offspring and now, and now? Instead, an abyss of grief, the dark place of the soul, the emptiness of a dead baby, but hers had not been a dead baby. This was worse. This was a baby killed. Herod-like the economic machine decreed all male children of this breed on common everyday farms are to be killed at birth. How could that be called farming? Where and when did this trend in farming start?

Surely when this relationship between man and

beast was first begun every calf would have been treasured. The cattle sheltered from the worst of the weather and the summer grass, prolific in its season, dried and stored, to be placed as precious fodder in front of their cattle. Milk and meat were the exchange, that part had not changed – but what had?

The respect for the modern day animal seemed to have gone, dissipated over time as people become more and more remote from the benefits they receive from this source. Peter pondered his fate; he was complicit in this hunger for everything cheap, cheap, cheap and endlessly available. He was one of the few at this end of the food chain, supplying the raw material. No, he corrected himself, he personally was never in the position to be supplying any of the raw material.

He thought through the line that his cow's milk now took. Farm to tanker to processing plant to outlet to consumer. Nothing very complicated in such a statement, but that is four distinct moves, each stripping away a layer of reality, of being in touch with where that milk was actually created, not manufactured. This cow, his cow, Number 476 had sacrificed her baby, unwittingly and certainly unwillingly to provide for him, here on the farm where that milk was counted in litres per cow. Yes, still at least in touch with her, then, onto the tanker where the milk was probably counted as a percentage of that driver's run and yes, his farm would still be mentioned, perhaps in code form, on some sort of paperwork. A tenuous link to his girl, the one who, this morning gave straining painful birth and then sacrificed her calf. The milk, just a sloshing part of a process in a huge, clean, sterile factory would be broken down, separated into the watery bit and the fatty bit, become a general measurement on a computer printout, more remote from his girl, his grieving girl, still hurting, physically bruised from birth and still ineffectually searching her stall for the baby she hoped to find hidden in a corner, something that was never going to happen for her, never going to be resolved for her except by forgetfulness, but do cows forget? Can cows forget?

Her milk now whirring in several directions at once, that magical substance made to sustain life, torn apart by centrifuge, whirled into constituent parts, heated fiercely, cooled fiercely, stripped of its own life as surely as her calf had been stripped of his life. The journey of calf ended in that illegal grave on the farm, the journey of this milk turning into someone else's luxury. No longer recognisable for its original purpose. Bagged and packaged to forget the origins on a humble farm, transformed into a commodity to be marketed to the highest bidder or worse, used as a loss leader on some anonymous shelf. And did that recipient even realise or know or care about the calf?

This bothered him, the lack of respect and his part in the whole process. Was there anything he could do or say to change things? He could think of nothing except accepting defeat in the face of the monster created in the name of efficiency and affordable food.

This week was even harder than usual for him. It held memories, ones that usually he held in check, behind a sort of frame or barrier of resigned inevitability. Grandmother had died a year before the calf incident, so could not at all be blamed or brought to account for it but somehow evoking her memory clashed up together with this other, the worst day of his life. Perhaps it was because he knew just how sad she would have been at the treatment meted out on her farm. It was her farm still in his eyes, even though he was the sole worker, and there were family interests in the farm, her name and character was written all over it.

She had been the one in her earlier years to plan and refurbish the barns, now looking somewhat used and tawdry and he had been the one to do his best to preserve them. Regular coats of stinking creosote, one of the many summer jobs he had attended to in his youth and beyond – there was no problem there. He loved to see a completed job. It was just strange how these sheds, always referred to as 'the new sheds' looked so old fashioned, tiny even. His was an older tractor, just for yard work and draying stuff around the farm, any serious tractor work was now handed over to contractors. He couldn't manage it all now anyway but when he looked at their monster equipment he marvelled, there certainly was no room in his sheds to park that machinery up under cover. Still, this is off the point, Peter's mood of despondency lay heavy on him, the incident, it brought him such a sense of shame, and this was Grandmother's anniversary. He felt he should be remembering her with the true sense of love and respect that he held for her.

It was she who stood up for him when he demanded the right to take his own way in life, to continue the farm. Parents were no longer on hand to guide and teachers desperately tried to steer Peter into a university education. It suited them to have the bright ones going down that line. It was the trend, but Peter had never been swayed by trend, he did what his heart told him was right and

Grandmother had stood up for him. She said, 'You try it my dear. The option to give up is always down the line and you are a useful boy, a handy lad, you'll get work round here always, my son – give it your best shot, son. You'll see, you'll make it work.' Having made that decision, he defied the educators who shook their heads and told him he was missing an opportunity. He had stuck to his guns, gone at the farming with energy and enthusiasm, but it was so hard to make it work financially. He put the hours in but could not earn enough to make the improvements he craved. Grandmother backed him as best she could but she was getting frailer in everything but the sharp wit and mind she had always held.

She spoke openly to him about how she felt it was no longer fair on the animals. How the farming had got out of hand and was being pushed in an unnatural direction. She could see no great logic in all the centralisation, the huge miles covered transporting food, and forage and straw around the country. It all seemed such a backward move in her eyes. Given the chance to make a resigned difference she would have organised food hubs, as the modern people would call them, local groupings of serious amounts of food, feed, fodder, keep it in the farmers' hands, share out the sales and buying within that group. Keep the shops supplied from close by. Why not? Where is the problem with that? Making a biscuit factory in the locality was not that hard. This runaway expanding beyond the boundaries of the farm only meant buying in what used to be done on the farm and left the poor farmer at the mercy of the salesman. The salesman was pushed by his next partner up the chain to present a graph with an upward slope, by which time the poor farmer was off the bottom of the chart translated into a blue dot if he was lucky and a red one if not. Grandmother saw it but had no power to do anything about it. Peter felt it but had no energy to do anything about it.

Going to visit somebody off the farm was a major effort for Peter, but there was somebody who he had pledged that he would take time to see whatever else he had to forgo. She did not live far away and she had been a friend of the family for as long as he could remember. He supposed that she had been his mother's friend, possibly the age thing worked out, but to Peter she was simply Margaret, not Maggie or Marge or any of the derivatives of that fine name but the full package – Margaret. He loved this woman, held her in awe, for beside the fact that she had brought up many children, none of her own, he found her to be a woman of wisdom. She understood what to say to Peter when no one else did and she never put upon him to buck up or do anything that felt beyond him. Peter was naturally a shy lad, an upbringing on a farm with few people to interact with can breed shyness and no matter what confidence Peter had in a situation with his animals or a practical problem to solve, once he was surrounded by people he shrank.

Margaret was his tonic, she made him feel safe and was probably the person he most opened up to about his immediate problems, but he didn't see it like that. Peter thought he was visiting Margaret for her sake, her poor physical health meant she didn't go out very much and despite having fostered many children, most had moved far away and those close-ish popped in, but not regularly. Peter was her regular visitor, coming every Monday, calving excepted, and any other time he happened to pass by he popped in for a how-do-you-do?

The relationship went something like this. Peter's kindliness prompted him to deliver a handful of fresh eggs, or a loaf of bread if he had gone for some for himself; Margaret smoked like a trooper and he kept her smoking cupboard topped up. There was no disapproval here, Margaret had always smoked, she smelled of smoke and her house was yellow from the smoke of ages. All this was invisible to the pair of them. When Margaret and Peter were together another thing happened to both of them. They spoke; they spoke about things that nobody else in Peter's life ever mentioned. Even Grandmother, that down to earth stalwart of farming life with a belief system that embraced common sense and kindness and polite sensitivity to all of Earth's creatures, be it man or beast of field and forest (possibly an exception made for rats and troublesome mice – they didn't need her help). Although helping him and being there to talk through the farming day, week and year, Grandmother did not step beyond those boundaries. Margaret did, and he loved these times with Margaret.

Firstly, she told him about her 'visits'. To Peter, who remembers Margaret's stories from since he was a child, they were just that, stories. But as Peter matured he realised that Margaret was actually telling him her experiences and because of the gradual nature of his realisation he had not stopped Margaret to question her about these 'stories'. It was far too late for that anyway, Peter was under the spell of the wonders that his best friend and confidante could elucidate to him. In all the dark days that Peter travelled, this was his one point of light in the week, his weekly couple of hours spent with Margaret, smelly Margaret, and he loved it.

'My boy, let me tell you about the time I flew to a cave. A cave that opened out onto a wide, wide vista and there I was visited by a Being of Light. This Being told me that I was allowed to come with her. It was a Her, the best of them are. They pick you up my son and fly you, I loved the feeling, flight, like a bird, but without the flapping and she took me up, up and along and all the stuff around me got hot with a special kind of non-burning heat and I was in it and it kind of melted away my outsides and then I got to look inside myself, and there was lots of love and I saw my children. The ones who had been with me, Tommy and Ivan and Gregory, I mostly had boys, and they grinned and waved and said thank you to me for being their mum for just a while, and that felt wonderful because they hadn't done much of that when I had them here under my feet, smashing things up and taking the mickey and getting into trouble at school – but there I could see the real them, the bits of them that really mattered, the bits that I had helped along and maybe just something that I did with them; the stories read at night, the safe home to come back to, the dinner on the table every night, no matter what they had done or where they had been creating mischief, was something that had pulled them through and I was glad that I did it.

'Sometimes I had had enough and thought I'd stop it with the boys. It was bloody hard, little buggers at times. You knew some of them Peter, they weren't always nice to you, I know that but you kept coming, drawn in by them because they were boys and you are a boy, but Peter you are different. You know Peter, it will catch up with you one day. You are different. Anyway at this place, the one I flew to with Her, she showed me a great big heart of something. I don't know what but it pulsed and shone and boy did it feel good, really special and I wanted to stay there, but she said I still had stuff to do and I had to go back, what I was being shown was like a thank you, something to keep me going a bit longer. That was ages ago and I went on some more. I had more boys, the bad ones, I got those ones that others didn't really want. I guess the social workers looked at my house and thought "well they can't wreck it any more, it's pretty crumby already".

But it wasn't the house that those boys came for it was the regular love.

'I loved those boys and the more they acted like they didn't love me, the more I gave them love, dinner always on the table and a hot water bottle in a cold bed. That's what a home feels like son.'

Peter listened in awe to these stories. They came thick and fast from Margaret, and she smoked, puffed away on her cigarettes like there was no tomorrow. She gave those boys of hers love, she didn't expect them to stay for a long time, or to show gratitude or thank her because she knew deep down that this was exactly the treatment they needed, it was all she could do, and since she lived in the country, the land would just have to do the rest.

There was a tree swing outside and footballs in various states of fullness or puncture, a couple of bicycles that had been donated along the way and the countryside to roam. These were mostly city boys, youngsters, and she took them in with their rough and swearing ways and she conquered them from the inside out, and the little part of them that Margaret mended never ever went bad again. She did her bit with love.

Some of Margaret's tales felt fantastical – Peter held them all in his heart, he didn't remember them word for word but he gleaned the essence of them. He would sit with Margaret, sometimes it would be in winter and there would be a fire on in her meagre house, boys in various stages of unrest, anger, or gradually succumbing to her strange powers of transformation would be there too. They would be at the table, Margaret smoking as usual, one or other boys playing with cards, maybe a game of Patience or building a house of cards, keeping themselves amused in the dim light of the house with the flickering fire for warmth and comfort, another log and the cat. Margaret always had a cat, or two and once the city boys had finished with their torturous ways, or the cat had fought back well enough for them to call it a truce then there would be a cat curled up on a chair or someone's knee. Margaret talked and smoked, she didn't really ask anyone to listen or pay attention and it made it kind of easy. She stroked a cat, smoked a cigarette and burbled on about this or that. Sometimes it was about school. The school bus went past in the morning and the boys were meant to go to school. They mostly did, but sometimes, well, it didn't happen and Margaret would just be gently chatting about schools and how it's a good idea to get the reading sorted so you understand what's going on, not being left behind. Just little pointers to be dropped into these stray lads' minds to let them know about important stuff in life. Somehow she managed to enthuse them just enough to make them want to make the effort to achieve here in the countryside, when they hadn't been able to do in the city. Here there was no pressure to be 'cool'. There were no gangs other than the house full at Margaret's and the ones who had already had the treatment, the quiet love, the hot dinners and the gentle persuasion were slightly tamed. This rubbed off on the next bunch coming through this system. As one boy left, Margaret would be gifted another. The social workers valued Margaret in a hands-off manner. They were amazed at her capabilities; somehow it didn't conform to their textbooks but as long as there was space with Margaret they were keen to get one of their charges a place.

Peter shared this upbringing. He could not remember a time when Margaret had not been in his life. She had finished with foster care now. He supposed the boys were the ones he had come to see but he never stopped his visits to Margaret anyway. The foster boys stopped, but Peter continued and as Margaret had become frailer and probably weirder he became her biggest point of contact with society. She had never cared what people thought of her, she certainly rowed her own boat, ploughed her own furrow or whatever simile you want to use. She was neither poor nor well off, she just saw no reason to change things, so she didn't. As long as she had her basic food and cigarettes she was happy. She had the cats and Peter and she lived with the seasons. If it was hot she wore her stockings round her ankles, if it was cold she wrapped up in anything she could lay her hands on. No fashionista here.

Chapter 3

*Inheritance issues may cause a feud and
ruin Peter's livelihood.*

Ok then, he thought. If Life is taking me down this
road I had just as well acquiesce and take it on the
chin. However has it come to this? He wondered.
Once I was a happy soul, I always knew that farming
was for me. As a child I played in amongst the barns
and climbed on the hay, sneaking through passages
made high up in the hay barn, smelly, sweaty and
dusty but so much fun. Creating games with the
animals, the farm cats curious but afraid to be
caught, their little faces poking through the gaps
between bales, us on behind them determined to
trap them and make them be our friends. One or two
allowed a tentative stroke but take it too far and they
were off like a shot. All this caused uproarious
laughter, just a few pals round to play and we spent
hours wandering from field to field poking sticks in
holes hoping we would disturb a rabbit or better still
a fox or badger. Sometimes it was just the challenge
of tracing the river back up the valley to see where it
might lead and the excitement of finding a sheep,
long dead and now disintegrated, just bones and the

vestiges of a ragged wool coat straggled in between the boulders of the river. Oh how that gave us amusement, and possibly, unbeknown to us at the time, a lesson in anatomy!

Peter was thinking to himself. 'This is such a paradox, I know I am in the right profession, I love my job, I love farming, it is such a necessary part of the economy, it makes perfect common sense to be producing a commodity that every living creature needs – food. But, and this is a huge BUT! must I do it like this? It is the sad feeling of being forced along lines I would not take myself. Why must I sell my calves away off the farm? I like the calves, I could happily look after them here if only I had time and it made sense financially. Instead I have to make every available space into another shed for the cows. More cows, more cows, more cows. The farmers who are getting out are shedding animals like old skin and I am being forced into restocking. Must I do it like this? I have no time to think, I am tired and weary now.'

It is a sorry state when a family affair causes angst. Peter had been lucky in his dealings with his sister and her part in the family affair. She was not interested in the farming side of the family heirlooms but was interested to know whether her grandmother had left any treasures, perhaps family jewellery. After all, that was how the previous generation accumulated riches, a nice brooch or ring was much prized. Peter had never thought about this aspect of the family fortunes and although he had been the closest to Grandmother, it was because of their affinity for the practical job of farming. She rarely got dressed up beyond her smarter skirt and jumper for a church visit and those had latterly been funerals more often than weddings. The youngsters had taken a turn away from traditional church weddings so there had not been any local occasions to fire up on all cylinders for.

There was no safe in the house, no tickets from bank vaults came to light after Grandmother was gone, just the old fashioned store of hats, coats and clothes. Peter would not be redesigning the kitchen or changing the furniture, maybe the very old battered sofa could go but otherwise he felt no need for big changes and in any case the everyday work of farming, on his own, took up every ounce of his energy.

It was not his sister but cousins that were causing a stir. This same grandmother had other grandchildren from a different branch of the family. They had appeared at the funeral, a quiet one held at the local church with a vicar who had barely known the family and who spoke rather perfunctorily, listing Grandmother's life story haltingly and without genuine feeling. The wake in the village hall was run by some of Grandmother's long-standing friends and there were reintroductions to a few distant (in terms of both miles and smiles) cousins who had really come to find out what there might be to glean.

The idea of a farm in the family brought a very wrong idea to the surface. Those away from the realities of farming life may consider that to be a landowner of any sort automatically puts the family in the ranks of 'the rich' but this is not necessarily the case. Farms have buildings and a farmhouse and fields and hedges and ditches and electrics and water pipes and lanes and costs. The days of rich pickings in farming were long gone and although a farm is a decent asset, it cannot be cashed in and stay as a workplace for the farmer. It cannot be used as collateral unless there is a new or different form of income to pay for borrowings against the farm and every farm takes maintaining if it is to hold its value. Many farms were on the market, farming being a difficult profession, one of trends and price hikes due to fluctuations in world grain and oil prices, and, of course, the weather. No matter how careful the farmer, the returns were not assured to be on the rise year on year. For all these facts, something that Peter knew first hand, and his sister understood second hand through her contact with Peter and Grandmother, this knowledge did not extend beyond that inner circle and cousins, feeling that their relationship to Grandmother held as much weight as Peter's, asked questions of inheritance.

This subject had not arisen before. Peter had worked hard alongside Grandmother and looked after her as much as she had looked after him. It was a symbiotic relationship, an unspoken partnership and nobody had looked into the future, the day to day business taking up all the time for the conversation that there was. It was with dismay that Peter realised why these long distant cousins had appeared out of the woodwork. He barely remembered them, apart from as names on a Christmas card and now here they were in the flesh. There had been no visit to the farm, the funeral was at the church and the wake, straight afterwards in the village hall. Their idea of farm and farming an unrealistic honey pot.

The funeral obligations over, Peter returned to the farm to continue with his daily tasks. His sister had borne the brunt of questions about

Grandmother's wishes and she had nothing to say. It was too soon for this sensitive part of the family to be thinking in terms of goods. They were grieving the loss of the family matriarch who had held everything together in practical terms and acted as mother and companion to Peter and his sister. The space she left was gaping at that moment and raw and real to these two. Life returned to a sort of normal. Routine for Peter was what saw him through the next dark days. Lingering in the back of his mind was the thought of having to sort out a mess of inheritance and he didn't know what the outcome might be. Meanwhile, day after day passed and the subject was not broached, neither did any family rings or brooches come to light. A fleeting thought just passing through.

Take this short time to familiarise yourself with Peter's situation. He has been given an ultimatum by his heart. It cannot bear the pain being placed in front of it on a daily basis. He has made mistakes that have cost him and his beloved cows their dignity and in one case her child. He feels all this so acutely now. His sleeping, something that used to be a 'given' in Peter's life is now being stormed by turns of wakeful worrying and noisy racket, all things that are new, like something is boiling to a peak. Peter is alone, nobody to talk to and no way to allow the head of steam to be released. What pressure is cooking up from the dark depths of his soul? He is contemplating a terrible sin, an outcome so dreadful that he cannot think straight. He has thought through simply getting rid of everything, closing the whole farm down, calling in the clearance guys, those folk from the auction house who line up your life in lots, matching up a mildly desired object with what appears to be tat. But for Peter, that tat would be his life and his memories. There are boxes and boxes of old equipment, too outdated to be considered anything but scrap and rubbish to anyone else, but to Peter it represents the memories of a grandfather who looked after him and taught him how to work through a mechanical problem to its scientific conclusion. Taught him patience and allowed him to use his tools, bought him piecemeal a toolkit of his own. Those skills had been vital once Grandfather was gone and he became main fixer and doer around the farm.

To consider seeing those old tools, no longer sharp and keen, unlike the memories Peter still held in sharp focus, to contemplate seeing them lined up in collapsing cardboard boxes, rained on, exposed, for junk vultures to pore over. No, that could not be.

Peter's life could not come to an end like that. To consider an end, an end to what? An end to a career spanning only a few decades, one that should be ongoing, the type of career that should be measured in generations not lifetimes. This little farm that had before him down the ages been supportive in its fields and farming soul to many, many people. Had seen children and adults and the older generations swing their way through. Yes change had taken place, modernisations, but in such a manner that still there was life to be lived and lives supported. The land had not changed so much that it could not, with care, still make that support, be that solid scaffolding holding up an extended family, with wings outstretched into the community supporting on those wings many other's needs for milk for their family cups of tea, meat for their meals around a table. A table where conversation, the news of the day was passed over and here was Peter, at the end of the line. No one at his table, no one to be able to chat through the triumphs or tribulations of his day. What would Peter do now? Where would this sad scene leave him, still stubborn, not desirous of an end that allows the vultures of life to rip away what small dignity he held for himself? What of his ambitions, his hopes?

His hopes, the last of the fairies from Pandora's box. Without hope there was nothing, but Peter was a farmer and he had the cows to see to and the calves to feed, so he wearily, tired now from lack of good sleep, girded up his loins once more and headed out to do his duty by those animals. Could he do the deed that played around his head? Not today, there are animals to tend.

––––––––––––

The goo is on the move. Through county and town it trundles on, hardly a problem in most places, just treated as an unusual stain on buildings or pavements here and there, unnoticed even. The food industry had all but clobbered it with their small-scale items being easily immunised, the goo neutralised by production, but in other areas where the loads were large and the ingredients dusty there was still an ongoing problem to sort out, and, of course, these conditions were the ones encountered on farms, Peter's being no exception.

The story so far. From the chundering and vibration of a ship's hold to countryside farms, hoppers and pits, was one of continual movement for the tiny parts of this goo. They were totally unaware of their journey, unless the temperature or moisture content changed then all came to a halt, or conversely, speeded up beyond the everyday workings of time. Exponential growth, fast forwarding at a rate beyond control has fascinating potential. The first split had created a doubling, slightly smaller in weight but potent. Even more potent than the original split was the one from the second generation atoms, after all they now were working with a memory of that first split, whereas the very beginning had been a trial. Possibly a trial that would have turned upon itself straight away and fizzled out, a damp squib of evolution, a dead end, cul-de-sac, never to be tried again, for those perfect conditions for the first movement out of staticity would never ever be encountered again. No one could replicate the many factors of engine and vibration, warmth and moisture. But are we taking into account the exact orientation of the ship at the moment of that birth? The place and strength of the magnetic quality of the earth, which may well be a factor. Ask atoms, they love magnets and in turn a magnet is but a small portion of electricity. Was exactly that magnetic pull needed? Or was it the placing of the moon on that day that shifted the moisture or sea or wave to create such a perfect storm of events for that first tiny change that had never before happened on the earth? Is this in fact, where we all came from? How we built our bodies, once, a very long time ago? Is it credible that this problem, now being carted around on wheels and in the back of lorries, is a forced kind of evolution speeding to a different perfect home, that once upon a time, it would have taken many millions of years to find?

Now we have the first split, evidence of this possibility lies in our very being and that of leaf, and tree and beast and feast of food all around, but the second split, this one, the one with memory of the first split, this one holds the intelligence.

Think about it. First one, chance, change because of a lining up of conditions unreplicable since the nuances are unknown. The second split, memory, no longer needing the absolute perfection of condition because it has already happened once. Yes, the basics, the warmth, the moisture, the food whatever that is, but the range has widened now. The plus and minus of the event window expanded enormously, because this goo is alive, can make it out of the hold of the ship, away from the engine noise and chunder. It has already evolved that much and is loving it, or is it? Can this process be said to have those feelings, love? A feeling, attributed to humans, and what about the cows? The bull and the cow, drawn together by hormonal reaction and receptivity, in that wish, that desire for reproduction. Can we attribute that perfect mating to produce a little calf like the one that Peter had to kill just born? Can we attribute that to love? To nature taking her course further up the evolutionary path than our little atom of goo, now making waves for itself along the journey, splitting because it now knows how to. Just like our cow and bull need the warmth of the sun to grow their food and the ability to come together at exactly the correct time in their season of splitting, of reproduction with that impetus of love. Cow love for the big necked bull, him glad of her company, heads low together, a smell, a step towards each other. Love, cows in love. Coming together for that time considered pleasure in the human world. Is it less pleasure in the world of a cow? Or even in the world of an atom, growing into a cell? Who are we to say that in his world, the atom's world, that his is not pleasure or at least achievement? Do we not love our achievements? We achieve and then we give prizes to those whose achievements we hold in high esteem.

Here, tiny atom, what have you achieved? You have changed and remembered that change to your children. It is the same trait we attribute to the learning in all other species. We learn and then we teach our children. Oh is our world any different whether it is large or small? How can we make meaning of scale? Here we all live in this huge universe, uncertain and unknowing of our place in it, unable to divide or devoid our feelings from our bodies. Unable to know what another, no matter how close and tied we are in our everyday lives, is thinking or truly experiencing even the self-same moment and event that we are. None of these things are we party to. But let us leave these deep thoughts and rise again to our everyday world.

This young woman, as Margaret was once, had come a long way in her beliefs over the years. She had not always been a foster carer; previous work for her had been in nursing, in hospitals. She had a naturally caring nature, and nurses put up with the less pleasant smells and sights of the world with equanimity and dignity. Margaret, once she had finished with that part of her career, had fallen into the care world quite easily. Sharing her home, at first had been quite tiresome. Her routine felt shattered as she suffered disrupted sleep patterns with strangers wandering about the upstairs landings in the night, walking the barricades of their new surroundings and feeling trapped themselves after their wild metropolitan lives, night owls many, with no instilled sleep patterns. Margaret had over the years come to view these poor patterns as a start to her training camp rules. Up all night is fine, do as little as possible to disrupt anybody else's sleep but then get up at a sensible time in the morning for a full day's activity. The fresh air life of walking and outdoor playing soon turned the owls into daytime birds and the unsightly dark rings of their city eyes into bright observant child's eyes, full of curiosity. Once down off the high horse of faked ennui at Nature's playground, they took an interest, bringing treasures to Margaret for identification or dragging her to the window to spot a creature or its habit and question why? Why? Why? Margaret made good food, plain, unfussy and she accepted help when she could. These boys at first balked at the tasks in the kitchen but Margaret's muttering ways soon inculcated them with the idea that the best chefs were male. Stereotyping did not hold in Margaret's world, she could wield an axe or a chainsaw as well as anyone and always had a sharper than sharp knife on her person. She gathered strange parts of plants, this was her nurse role, and made potions, ointments and general tonics, and a veritable cornucopia of drenches. Old fashioned maybe, but also effective, no children were ill under her care. They thrived, and the decency of one child, once allowed to surface from under the old skin of gansta slough, soon began to work its magic on the new arrivals. Dear Margaret, firm in her routine, unable or unwilling to take umbrage at any slight delivered by unfeeling words, signs or whispered comments, turned these little chaps into soldiers for good.

They were not going to repay her straight away; they did not understand the flow of life, the downward fountain of love from older generation to younger. That is a secret of age and experience. The teenage years where her charges were yet situated are ones of confusion, of know-it-all false confidence and an underlying uncertainty of gender, place and direction. Margaret was the pointer, the firm hand that turned them back again and again and again. Always there to say 'go this way my son, it hurts less this way'. Yes, hold the knife and feel the keenness of the blade but also understand the damage it can do and the flow of life is one way, a mistake made in a moment of uncontrolled anger cannot be undone. There are consequences to actions. Be easy on yourself, choose your actions with a clear head. Yes, hold the knife and feel its keenness but use the knife to cut the bread and gather fruits and it will never turn on you. Cut badly and you will be scarred forever. Thus her charges learnt.

Chapter 4

This man-made farmer, torn within; grits
teeth, decides, that he <u>will</u> win.

This morning came too fast for Peter; his internal alarm wakened him as usual at the early hour of 4am. It was still cold and damp from the previous dreary weather – there seemed to be run of it. Oh, for a brighter start to the day, the weather amplified his weary mood. At present it all felt like a slog. Nothing could break through this feeling dragging him down. The pit of his stomach ached with tearing grief and his head was in a mist, a fog of disbelief. If this is how life was driving him should he be the one to get out? Still the practical problem of how to do it? Peter's poor heart was aching; he did not even understand what was going wrong in his life. He could not have tried any harder, given any more effort or energy to the tasks placed in front of him but dark clouds were amassing around him. He had been given an ultimatum by the bank, no longer would they service his overdraft. It was their prerogative to call this in, part of an agreement he had made all those years ago when he had been promised by 'they money men' that it would all come right. 'You see now', 'the trends are on the up and up', 'world prices will soon ease the burden' and 'the opening of overseas markets' would take Peter's small offering of milk and meat from his farm into a new realm of wealth.

Well, it had not happened like that. Peter had increased the numbers of cows on the farm, doubled his hours in the milking parlour to accommodate this new trend and been rewarded with falling prices and extra costs. His girls had not enjoyed the cramped conditions he was now forcing them to live under. He could tell this from their drooped heads and petty squabbles round the feeding bays. The quality of the milk had reduced and with it his price per litre. He had more small-scale injuries and scrapes and bumps on the cows, ones that festered and were slow to heal, and his farm tracks had taken a beating with all the extra hooves marching up and down. All in all Peter was not enjoying this new regime. He had questioned the advisors, asked when things would take this turn for the better that they had promised him when he agreed to be part of their mega world plan to feed countries many miles away with food from his farm. It went against the grain at the time, seemed illogical to have such grandiose schemes on the go, but he went along with it because that was where the subsidy payments led and he needed them to service just the basic outlay of feed and bedding and bare maintenance on the farm. Now it was all falling apart around his ears, prices were slipping, but not for those in the offices, they might shed a few people here and there but their wages were stable, their vehicles got larger not smaller and their tentacles gripped him ever tighter. What would he do now? There was nothing to sell, to offer the banks, but he had each day to come up with feed and bedding and a serviceable vehicle to take his stock to market, or pay again for someone else to do it. My, what a fix, Peter! How will you get out of this one?

Part of him ached to leave it all behind and another part, the defiant Peter, the one who had eschewed all common sense to set himself up in the first place as a farmer still dug his heels in and KNEW deep down he could do this. There has to be another way, a different way. Others could follow their noses blindly; he would do something different, something radical. He now felt his grief turn to determination, his determination turn to steel and what had been pain now became the fodder, the nutrient to fuel him through whatever it would take to turn this situation around and give him a new start in life. He was not done yet. No way Peter, you are stronger than this. Throw shit at me, and I shall turn it to the very manure needed for my growth. This is not fighting talk; Peter had no fight in him. This was a personal struggle. He would go independent, he would stop listening to the 'wisdom' of those pushing farming from the outside, willing to put their own profits and livelihoods before those of the guys who did the graft. The manipulators and moneymen smugly working out how his life should be led and dropping him in it with a point nought one on a spreadsheet. Well no more, no thank you. He knew there was no point in fighting back, his was to be another way. He would melt out from underneath them. Pay his way out, shrink his stock, give up land if he had to, pull his horns right in. Honest farmers had tried to reason, to protest, to bring to the milk drinking public good reason for change but it all made tiny waves that soon died down. How can tired and busy people make their voices heard? Impossible.

Peter thought back to a time when he had the fun and excitement of planning a venture and getting all the materials together, having someone to talk things through with, discuss and down or up size as necessary, talk through the pros and cons of a situation – these small things were what was missing in Peter's life now. Loneliness, tinged with a sadness that his fortunes had not spread before him in a manner that he would have liked. Why? Was there anything that our man could do to change his own situation? At present he felt not, he felt trapped, and put upon by bank and contracts which he knew in his heart were not fair – how oh how had he slid into this sad situation?

Peter remembered when he had been having a problem on the farm with water pipes. It was the day Margaret had given him the book; he took it, even though he had not expected to read it. He needed to replace a trough in one of the far fields. It was not an easy job as the original water piping had been installed many years before, but he had two choices, find or buy a bowser and then have to lug and fill, another daily task which he didn't have time for, or replace the trough and test out where the old pipes went to ensure there were no problematic leaks. Where the pipes tracked through gateways it was fairly easy to see what sort of condition they were in, and he had already done the main of the work over the easy ground but sometimes the pipework disappeared underground and bushes had sprung up. This was not the kind of job where brute force would do the trick – with water meters spinning in the yard just for the day to day milking, washdown and general running of the farm, a breakdown in the far off fields just could not be countenanced. There was no spare money in the coffers for extra expense; every penny had to count mightily.

All this worry coincided with one of Peter's weekly visits to see Margaret. And it went something like this:

Peter, visibly weary, arrived at Margaret's door, he already had the shopping, another little task he had taken over, though Margaret did go out to the village she could no longer manage large loads of shopping, hence Peter's offer of assistance. He helped her put the tins and tea and cigarettes away in the same old cupboards that she had ever had and settled himself down at her table for his weekly chat. Mostly she talked at Peter, he was a man of few words by habit and the quiet on his farm had exacerbated that trait. Funny how Margaret always knew. Peter had a lot on his plate in any case but this water situation was an extra worry. He had heard about clever machines that the water board had that could detect leaks but if the problem was on his side of the water meter, then he was liable to pay. In any case he didn't have a leak, at least not yet. He had a new trough lined up ready to be plumbed into the field and he knew where the end of the pipe was. His problem was locating the pipes from the gateway to the trough. There may be no problem to solve if the old pipes had held, or were safely buried out of harm's way where no heavy cow hooves would break them and if they had been suitably covered up away from UV light, the plastic would still be strong. These were the things he needed to find out just for peace of mind before committing to the work. Timing was not on his side, he did need the cows to use that field since the grass was just right. Conundrum, conundrum.

Margaret made the tea, a pot, of course and placed a stained mug in front of Peter.

'What's up with you then, my son?' she asked.

Peter told her his conundrum and she squealed with delight.

'Oh let's sort that then.'

Peter wondered whether, at last, she was losing her marbles, but Margaret calmly reached down a piece of paper and a pencil and told Peter to make a rough sketch of the farm. She directed him to mark out the fields and then to draw all the pieces of water pipe that he knew about. His sketch was marked with a strong dotted line, for water pipe. At the farm end it was easy, the pipes headed out from the meter and through all the gateways where he or others had replaced the pipe overground when these stretches had in the past become brittle with age or failed with frosts. Then the trail went cold until he got to the place where the new trough was to be established.

Margaret muttered to herself and got out a big needle from her mending kit. It already had a thread hanging from it. She dangled the needle, holding it aloft by the thread end and traced it over the line of the pipe on Peter's makeshift map.

A strange thing happened, instead of hanging totally vertically as would be expected in any normal gravitational field, just like dear Earth possesses, the needle started to drag slightly towards the left, well, off centre to you and me, left is subjective. Margaret was pleased, she chuckled a little and said 'look, look' to Peter. The line of the needle crept along with Margaret's help but not guidance. It was rather like she was taking a tiny dog for a walk on a lead and allowing the dog to choose its own path. When it got to the field gate that Peter was most interested in, he was totally drawn in. The concentration on both Margaret and Peter's faces was intense; somehow they had breached the barrier of normal. Peter, who knew his fields well, was mentally in the field and he could trace in his mind that this pipe was laid round to the left of the field gate, an obvious move, but then it headed out into the field for a few metres and back to the perimeter of the field. A deep old drainage ditch ran in that direction and the needle dragged its way off the vertical leading along with the tip just ahead of the string of thread. It traced its way slowly along the length of the ditch. No more great surprises and the place of the trough-to-be was reached.

Peter scratched his head, why would it go away from the edge and back again, then he remembered, there was a big old tree stump just there. If someone was intent on burying the pipe, especially important near the gateway where many hooves converge, then it made sense to skirt around the big tree roots, back to the edge of the field and then dangle the pipe as deep as the ditch would allow, keeping it safe from cow legs and light.

Peter looked at Margaret, they had both returned from their relevant places of concentration and Margaret urged Peter to draw the revealed pipe onto his map. It did not occur to Peter to question what had just happened. This was dowsing, he just didn't know how to do it. Now he had seen dowsing in action he was convinced he could at least give it a try in the future.

Sure enough, when Peter returned home and had

a good rake about in the deep ditch, he came across the pipe, intact and in good enough repair to attach the new trough that day. Dear old Margaret, she had saved him a lot of angst and probably a load of money that he didn't have anyway. Thank you Margaret with your special skills.

'My life, this is an exciting book, so gentle and yet so feeling,' says Peter to himself. 'I thought I would not like it, but I'm desperate to find a way to get back to its chapters.' Peter mused, 'One day I would like to do what this chap has done, to sort out my life and make it my own again.'

Good for you Peter, are we all with him on this one? Is the world just too bossy a place for most of us these days? Are you allowed to make your own mind up? Make your own way in life or is it that there are so many different hoops to climb through, jump through, tick boxes to make your way through. Has business, any business, farm or otherwise, turned into an exercise in political correctness and box ticking before the business idea can even get off the ground? Whatever the idea is, be it a brilliant one ready to save the world or a basic food prep business, makes feeding the five thousand with loaves and fishes seem more achievable.

There is red tape, advice comes thick and fast

from professionals willing to give their tips and demand an hour's fee and officials come to straff the employer, straff the warehouse and shopkeeper. Plaster the walls in safety information for fear of reprisals, take out insurances to cover the unimaginable but do not dare to stray into the region of risk for there lies the no man's land of uncovered risk, but dare not claim, or the costs will rise against you next quarter, next year. Oh my, to start up on your own in anything bar the most timid of business is to drag with you the paid and willing-to-be-paid-for-nothing-good-or-concrete crew. Do you see them? Hear them calling at your door? Seeking out the easy option in life, seeking a way to keep one bony digital finger in your pie, in your bankroll, sorted to be able to swoop the money out at their own discretion, soft soaping their way around your business with impossible to decipher or remember acronyms, the PCI DSS types stealing from the grafters. We had them exposed in one area, PPI perpetrators, barely getting their comeuppance yet, and exposed, they set the face of the corporation 'sorry man' or better still 'sorry woman' to soften the blow while behind the closed doors of their offices more clever pants schemes are being cooked up. These low lives drag down the honest likes of Peter, sucking out monies and injecting tasks above and beyond the needs of farming.

The common sense man keeps his head low and is busy enough to stay in honest graft. Let us clear our ditches and layer our hedges neatly, allow the waters to drain and the stock to be secure and have the shelter from the wild elements they need. That is where the hours should be put, but no, we must see Peter, fiddling with his paperwork. Afraid to get behind with it but without help, either voluntary from within the family, or paid, from without. Fiddling with his forms and tags and lists and future field plans to keep up with this modern way of farming when his could be the long-handled shovel and billhook and an afternoon chopping out the firewood and tidying up the edges, the hedges, the surrounds that hold his little farm tight together. As the wind rips through the unlaid hedge and the water pours over the blocked up ditches and drains so also does the heart and life and love of his farm pour out through the edges of his bank account into accountant and insurance and rates and unnecessary bits and bobs. Oh Peter you are less suited to this task of paperwork and more suited to tend and care for the parcel of our sacred ground and you would so willingly do so. Let him go, let him go.

Peter catered for, for just a while, we leave him with a despondency to carry and no outlet other than to wallow and hover over his tiny calves, due to disappear into a future he is uncertain about and unwillingly he acquiesces, but we know this. However, do we know or understand what is happening within the tiny sphere that is our evolving atom? Looking within, we are drawn towards the spiralling vortex. Pulled down with a curiosity borne of previous experience, this funnelling and tunnelling effect has held us in its thrall before and will not disappoint this time; Peter also has an insight into this world. This is the world he is beginning to inhabit in his head space, he may access in a different manner, but then there are many roads to Rome and in the Infinity of Space many more. Importantly we travel, fast, whizzing and whooshing along, weightless and alone. Yet, expand your mind and feel into this space around you, are you actually ever alone? Or are you, with me, feeling the presences of myriad jolly chattering creatures, pleased to see you and meet you at last in their own territory? Those whose outer being you are meeting every day, stepping on and over, crying with and laughing with, the air, the energy of your daily life tied up with these, the tiny lives therein the physical being you call yourself. Are you with me, can you do that? Can you imagine yourself in two types of being at once? This one you think and read with and another that makes your body up, that sometimes seems out of your control with illness, or tiredness, or grief, or maybe even hunger, worse still, pulling you out of yourself with addiction.

Still here? Still with this theme? Whirling along having dived into the sensibilities of the tiny atom and finding that he is never alone, always in touch with the larger portion of himself. One yet many, feeling personal yet in a crowd. Like the majestic clouds of birds that sweep and swoop overhead in winter, never clashing but knowing – knowing what the next move is. Are you as clever as that? Do you know where that next move is? Evolution does, would like to take you swooping onward upward towards a better health, a better understanding of this world we all live in, all of us, human, animal, plant and every mineral. Have I missed anybody out? No, but yet we are all missed out if we do not attend to that part of us that is human, animal, plant and mineral, for that is where we have come from and we do not know where we are going unless we feel for it, extend the tentacles of our consciousness forth, stretch and make that inward seeking effort to feel for the next move, to sound out what evolution would be straining us to do. Like our little atom as we first met him, he did not know, he was and he strived.

Outdoors, away from the paperwork, the virtual paperwork, now assigned to shining screen and print-your-own copies, the trees on the farm are having their own revolution. This is something they are suited to and magically perform each year. Autumn is upon them and each in its own time's turn shrivels the last of its leaves to lend a bare twiggy hand to the sky. But life is not gone from the trees, only slumbering awhile whilst temperatures hold the living at a slower tempo. Still the protective bark sustains the life sap beneath and the wild creatures use the roots, trunk and branches as home. This colony lives in symbiosis, the idea for 'tree' having been laid down in the annals of evolution many millions of years ago. Still evolving, but on a needs-to basis, our oaks, ashes and hazelnuts stud the copse and hedgerow. While climate and chainsaw allow, these trees will last many years, support many habits and even in degeneration be useful, eventually to return, unblemishing their surrounds in any negative manner and they are made of the same stuff as humans.

What makes tree, Tree? Standing majestic, wood, crafted out of water and waste from his own fallen leaves. Clever – and life, yes from the sun and the water and the soil, but all trees have that. What makes this tree live? The myths give this job to The Sylvans, the spirit of the woodland glade. Dare you travel that road with me? Can you give Peter a spirit? Certainly a consciousness because how else could he feel so acutely? Peter has empathy, it resides there alongside his consciousness, for how else could he love his animals as much and next to that how can he feel along with them? This, the man who matches the grief of his own loss of child in the same breath as that of the loss to a cow of her calf. Here is a man who sees and follows the natural order of life, who across the species *can feel*. Can you? Dare you admit that in this book a little truth is appearing? That we are not separate from our surroundings. That made of the same stuffs, this part of us returns to the same stuffs. That our feeling world can cross the species barrier and feel along with other beings that we love: cow, dog, horse, tree, flower, plant and bee. This is not a mere projected love for the sake of it but a love that tugs at our innards, is joined alongside that being who is living in our cells. The one who signals hunger, pain, emotion at a clammy level, a joy that lightens and brightens the face with an inner glow. Admit you have also experienced these things. You may not be farmer but you are human and to be dragged down is to create a natural buoyancy which means should you be let loose, you will soar. Work on yourself to cut yourself loose, to trust yourself to know and do the right thing by that inner part that is crying to rise and give again to you exactly what you desire. Come now with me back to the tree, she stands majestic and beckoning with her wide open branches, she says come sit with me awhile like your ancestors did and use my trunk as a natural resting place, a shade from sun and rain. We thought together then and can think together again. Find your tree, your place, and farm yourself, re-attach yourself to the natural world and feel its pulse, its breath. This is where you will gather strength and succour, ideas, firmness, grounded reality under your feet. Try it.

Chapter 5

Benumbed with figures, zoning out, new problems looming. No way out!

Morning loomed again, too fast for our man, yet he knew he had to respond to the call of the alarm. His body, out of sheer habit, already sitting before even the third sounding of the abrupt bell had passed. Weariness hung over him, clung to him like damp rags and a feeling cut through his brain. This was not a morning he was going to enjoy. There were a couple of events scheduled into the farm diary, it happened every month, and like a schoolboy dreading a maths lesson, but realising the inevitability, gloom flopped his mood grimly.

His whole demeanour took on the heaviness of the tasks in hand. One cerebral, unwanted and likely to affect his mood and livelihood long term and the other a temporary pain but nevertheless severe and recurring like a bad toothache that clears up in bouts but is never resolved, therefore hangs in the background like a spectre waiting to scare again and again.

The first task, a visit from the farm advisor and

bank man. These two appeared, seemingly jolly, smart, fresh and clean. He really did not understand their cleanliness, it shone out of pink shirts and smart leather-bound laptops, clean shaven with neatly trimmed hair. Even when he smartened himself up to go out he never achieved this level of cleanliness, all washing powder fragrance and shiny shoes. These guys kept their wellingtons in the back of their vast vehicles, they were clean too! Of course they have to be, in the name of biosecurity, the buzz word of official farm visitors, but these wellies were so untested by muddy gateways and being trodden and scuffed in the day to day running of the real work of farming that they could be cleaned off, hosed down and splashed with a foul smelling disinfectant ready for another five or ten minute cursory tiptoe around someone else's yard. These guys were most at home once that part of their visit came to a physical halt at the kitchen table, as the politely inevitable tea or coffee was proffered, they unzipped their monstrous mean machines from their dinky little logoed up baglets and huffed and puffed their way into their kind of farming. Clean, screen and in your dreams buddy.

He just knew already that their demands were all about cost cutting, shaving off a little here, discussing a juggling jigsaw of which units of this balanced against that unit of something else would allow the flow of farm subsidy to continue. Oh yes, they would get their fee. That is all factored in, actually it doesn't even feature on the page, it is an unwritten rule. However else could they be in a farming related job and stay so clean?

Their words became a dull hum in his mind. Numbed with the figures he was back in the barn with the calves, it was their last few hours with him. Boy, he loved those little fellows, their turned up snouts, and spindly legs tested out in quick wobbly bursts of involuntary joy of living. Even though they had only had the comfort of a short time with their birth mothers, life sung to them and better still in a crowd. He loved to bed them down deep and snugly, scratch their heads and necks and rumps while he trained them to feed from the unnatural angle of the bucket feeder. He felt for these little creatures, whispered apologies under his breath at the unfairness of their lives, and worse still his unbearable part in turning those very wheels of his sad industrial mode of farming. It would have been no better if he were the one receiving the calves at the other end of their journey. That was not the point. It was this endless stripping away of mother and child, so much the wrong order in life, anybody's life: calf, sheep, human, cat, dog, monkey, elephant, hen, lion, whatever popped into his mind, all desired strongly, with a fierce will, a maternal instinct to LOOK AFTER THEIR YOUNG. His thoughts were there, with the calves, but his head was nodding, acquiescing with this couple of guys telling him how to run his farm. Tapping and swiping at the glowing screens in front of them, commenting to each other from time to time in some gibberish jargon that left him cold. No, his feelings, his sentiments were outside in that barn with the next group of calves to go off, hustled un-understanding into a lorry to judder to their next destination. He did not know where or with whom. Would they end up on a kindly farm? Or just as another commodity kept to the minimum standards, alive but soulless, dead in the eyes, he had seen them like that and it pained him. Oh dear this is not a good day.

'They money men', as he called them to himself, rose, their cutting knives repacked into neat square computer packages and tucked under their arms. They offered a handshake, soft and weak at the elbow. His, a crusty strong leathery hand, wide as a paddle and one that had conveyed love and kindliness in every stroke of a calf's neck – he tried to mimic the way a mother cow licks her calf, he noted the pressure, the deep long strokes, the rubs against the grain of the hair. Not visible but penetrating, his connected sensitivity from hours of side by side living, here was a man truly 'at one' with his animals, sharing in their pain of separation. Oh God, does it have to be like this?

The men were gone, he had supplied the water, they had brushed off their boots, dipped them in their magic solution and with a clean biosecure wave of a hand were off to confuse and bemuse another salt of the earth farmer. Get him a 'best deal' from the subsidy packages on offer. They were 'in the know', had a 'finger on the button', an 'eye for the next trend'. Keeping these farming types' 'best interests at heart', while the heart of this farmer, our Peter, was sinking, sorry and sad with the responsibility of being part of these tiny lives and having no control over them beyond the scant few days in his care. He wished he could keep them, take them through to kill weight, see them grow, know and understand the strengths and weaknesses of the lines he bred. He could make better, more rounded decisions if he saw the whole picture. He would be proud to take good fat stock to market knowing he had taken them on their whole journey. But it was all so split up these days – specialising, they called it. Either you afforded a unit to grow calves or you afforded a parlour to milk cows – and time. How could you put time to both those operations? Impossible, so it all got split up. The calves had to go; in fact here was the lorry now. He mustered up his best jolly banter for the driver and joined in with the circus that was his life. Another unhappy clown.

Now what pained Peter alongside this was the inner knowledge of what separation from a child really felt like. His marriage had been a swift one, a sweet, short affair unfortunately to end too soon for Peter and the daughter who had been born here on the farm but soon removed, alongside her mother who could not manage the farming life. The long hours and smells and sights of the farmyard were not in her blood. The holiday romance turned serious when consequences of a pregnancy were taken into account and had not lasted the test of time, or the extended family living that those in farming situations are used to. Privacy and a small undetermined two-bed flat, with unknown neighbours and her own family close enough for comfort but far enough to feel some independence were where his daughter was taken. The city outskirts where coffee shops and hairdressers and shopping malls entertained with loud signs and posters, whirling beacons of modernity a million miles away from that fateful holiday cottage on a quiet lane. Entertainment in the local pub being the closest thing to metropolis living, had bound this woman to Peter but just for a short spell. Had he sensed her unease at the quiet? He no longer remembered, but he had felt all the pain and grief of separation from a child that he knew was his own and he had no power to protect or hold or love except from afar. He could not visit, the distance was too great and he had no one to care for his animals if he left the farm for more than a four hour spell. She was essentially lost to him, this baby of his, never to know his physical love, solid hugs and sweet times missed with a man who was her blood father. It pained him still. These feelings mingled with the pain of ripping the calves from their mother's sides so quickly, so soon, before even nature had finished with the proper act of birthing.

Into the earth, the calf's body was returning, not quickly enough because it was dry stony ground where Peter had done this last deed and his scarred heart still raw, for it was his desire to keep the beloved line from his favourite girl alive that had backfired. He had hoped that her female calf, should it have happened that way, would be part of his comfort for years to come. The lifespan of his cows was shorter than the cows he had been brought up with. Genetics had forced the milk sac to enlarge at the expense of the general good health of the whole cow. Peter was not convinced that the economics really did stack up when he was forced to replace cows more often than before, but as usual he had been caught up in what was a trend, and for replacement milking cows, the sperm available from bulls had been chosen for milk production, nothing else was available.

Artificial insemination was the norm now; few kept a bull for their milking cows. There were nice solid meat breed bulls around and they were seen in the fields calling to their cows, or anyone, within their booming lowing voices' range, and cows would sidle up to the great big necked manliness of the bull and coyly rub her head, in love for the time of her season. Peter so enjoyed watching these love affairs take place, seeing the relationship develop with the rising of the hormones and the knowledge that a calf was being conceived out of a type of natural love rather than a necessity and imposition for a cow standing in hope of a real mate but getting a gloved hand and a cold straw of semen cheated out of a bull on some distant genetics farm. Sad, sad times when love counts for nothing in the animal world. How might this diminish the end article? Peter wondered this himself and still tortured his mind over the little calf whose loveless conception had also his added guilt laid over it. The little calf, huddled under stony ground not even rotted enough as yet to return to the ground as fodder for the grass his mother may yet chance to eat. Sad, sad days indeed.

This new rule, disinfection points at the gateways onto all public highways put more strain on Peter. It was bad enough coping with his own few runs out in his vehicle but what about the rest of it? The postman could no longer come down the lane to deliver, so he had had to set up a 'secure' post box on the roadside. This meant, instead of a two minute chat with Postie, he had to make the effort to collect the post, another job. He no longer knew whether there was any post, and to make certain he had to go and look. It used to be simple, no postman, no letters that day. Deliveries were much more complicated. Drivers, still under the same pressure to deliver on time, wanted him to come to the end of the drive too! The curse of the mobile phone. He was summoned from his daily tasks. He changed the routine, getting up even earlier in order to at least complete the undisturbable milking in peace. This scattered his brain, dropping new ideas into an already overloaded mind. Peter's natural sense of order, his desire to do the best at every job he attempted was being eroded. He would find half done jobs, calves unfed and crying, taps not turned off properly in his haste to drop everything and rush to the end of the lane. He set up a box for small parcels but since many farmers were doing the same there had been a spate of casual thefts. Word had got about, he could not afford to be losing items and he never ordered anything unless it was totally necessary. A hose for the tractor, some small parts for the milking parlour all very necessary to keep things moving along, without them jobs were done badly or with great difficulty.

But outside something on the farm was growing. It crept silently in amongst the circles of hull and shell of the wheat that had earlier been delivered. Not good, Peter, beware Peter, infiltrators within the fragile stockade of the farm. How shall he deal with this new influx of disaster due to hit our man when he is already down? The papers had been full of it, some explanations blamed poor biosecurity on farms, some more sensible sources quoted trade routes as a legitimate place to begin a search for how this new monster was let loose. Either possible answer was never going to address the immediate problem to be faced by Peter. Finances already in trouble he could not be expected to throw away precious income along with this most recent delivery. What must the man do? At present he was still unaware, still rub eyed and reeling from his meeting and his loss, certainly not fit to face another problem.

There was a feeling of doom hanging over the farm; Peter, although having stated his determination to find a way through this, was weakening. How could he weather this new storm coming his way? He kept up to date as best he could with the events on nearby farms and knew his feed company was as likely as any other to be delivering feed tainted with this invasive goo but he had no particular back-up plan other than to keep a wary eye out and hold disinfectant in store. How could he keep himself safe? There were fines for those farmers not abiding by the new biosecurity rules and these threats added to his general angst. He needed another way, a better understanding in order to salvage what he had left in terms of self-esteem, some way to see a positive side to being alive, for at this time there was nothing, nothing that could alleviate his pain.

And where might we ask is the other way? Is there a universal pot of knowledge to be tapped in a situation such as this? Is there a tide sweeping along that points to a different path to take? Have we done with inhuman solutions to human problems? Can we get better at finding solutions ourselves? Ask a machine to count numbers, add, subtract, divide. Computation and permutations, those are the skills of the machine. The pure mathematical answer by itself does not address the complexities of lived life whether that life is lived by a large or small model. Humans need problems solved by fellow empathic humans, and sparky little atoms, creeping into existence do not consider themselves a problem at all.

Chapter 6

*Cringing Peter, market bound to face the
masses all around – he's terrified, but others
see good bones and opportunity.*

Here lies the book, open at the page he left it on
and drawing him in again to read its alluring
chapters. How can he have missed so much in his life
so far? Always so busy, always rushing, too much to
do in too short a time. And what had it cost him? His
marriage, his child no longer near enough to cuddle
good night every night and what for? He was no
longer happy but he loved his work. If only, if only
there could be a slower side to life. Time to think
through the problems and let him get to the bottom
of them not just skim over, mend it the best he can
for the day, only pay attention to the stuff that
earned the immediate money. The calf house needed
a total refurbishment if the next lot of calves were to
be comfortable but whenever would he have the
time and money to do it? He actually felt desperate,
his outer calmness could no longer sustain him and
he felt the pricking of tears behind his eyes.

'Please, please let me find another way. I really

can't cope with this pressure. I was not brought up to do half a job but now I am being forced by money concerns, and the feeling of being dragged down into debt, to cut corners. My lovely animals are losing their shine and I'm ashamed of them, I have to take them to market – how else do I pay my bills but I won't get the best prices and I laugh and joke with the other guys but it's all surface nonsense. I want my mum again – whenever did I say that last? Goodness I am 42 and I am crying for my mum. What on earth is happening to me?'

The back of his shirt was wringing wet with sweat; Peter had shoved and heaved with all his might, he was unable to bear the sight before him, and felt crazy with grief. Oh how can he ever look his animals in the eye again? This was like a sickness over him, he could not imagine how he had come to such a pitch but now he had started he just had to go on. The fire was raging, all the old wood he could find heaped up and set ablaze. This was the funeral pyre he had made for this calf. The burying had not gone well, the ground too dry and stony, his bank was empty and he could not call the renderers now for such a wrecked and rotted carcass; his walks had every day taken him past this poor burial ground for this cow's child, his sin, his decision, a poorly called gamble and this was the only solution he could think of. If he were to have a farm inspection, and there were such things now in place with the new disinfection rules, then his farm would have been deemed contaminated, a fetid carcass under the ground but not deep enough to be hidden. The tell-tale sight of circling bluebottles humming in the warmth of the day. They were not to be denied their food and farmed their children out on this poor wreck of a calf. It was disgusting, the heaving mass, transformed from beauty to the beast and Peter felt it, smelt it, and retched his way through this self-imposed torture. He must hide the evidence. He was hiding it from himself as much as from a would-be inspection. He needed to clean the ground, clean the air and blanch himself, purify himself from this sin forced upon him by circumstance, encroaching poverty and his desire for peace of heart for his favourite cow. All of it had backfired and wrong upon wrong piled up.

First the sinking feeling of there being a bull calf, when he had hoped for a heifer, then the necessity to take the pistol and shoot this calf. He had hidden it from its mother, she, still straining to rid herself of the placenta where this calf had been plugged into her life-giving sources and now, unplugged and undone, that tiny life, still beautiful. Born, killed, and buried all within an hour. Days later, the sin had not left him, not been resolved by those actions but reminded him every time he walked that path. A telltale smell haunting the air, sweet and sickly. Putrid flesh, what small flesh he had. His sin to be a skinny boy calf, not a breeder, allowed her skinniness because her bulging udder compensated that, but males of this breed, unwanted in the marketplace where no one would have them. Not unloved, for here on this farm there were two most willing to administer the love. Mother cow, already seeking, even while Peter was doing his best to alleviate her suffering by removing this calf killing from her sight. She heard it, whether she knew or understood. The noise was that, the death of her calf, and Peter, a man who loves his calves, would happily put in the hours to take care of such a sweet and gorgeous beast, snub nosed and cow eyed like his mum. Peter would have done that and with love but no, the dice had fallen wrong for all three. Calf dead, mother and Peter grieving and now Peter, his mind a blank of unforgiveness unto himself, unable to function and think. He gave over to function because his thoughts had already tortured him enough. His thoughts for his poor judgement and his guilt at what

Grandmother would have said or done. It was not squeamishness that made him retch, it was the wretchedness of the situation and the only solution he could come up with was this, the pyre where tomorrow there would be scorched bones. In tears of grief Peter scrabbled around for the last of the bedraggled skin and mess of what had once been his good idea and chucked it hissing onto the fire. He wiped his hands, but still they stank, and like Lady Macbeth, whose guilty spots of blood would not fade, Peter carried the stench of rotted and burning flesh with him to his bed that night and many others.

The end of the road for Peter's relationship with this particular bunch of cattle could not come quick enough. He loved all his animals but the pressure of keeping them in substandard conditions was really paining him. He knew he was not giving them the time they warranted. Too much else on was the excuse but really it had to do with the poor guy's feelings every time he entered the low barn. Head height was restricted at the far end, the stall fronts were a mish-mash of any old materials cobbled together to stop these poor dears escaping. Unfortunately they were standing right next to the slurry tanks and any run off tracked ahead of the doors and gateway so even when it was possible to allow them out to stand on the concrete for an hour or two, they were standing in muck. Not best for their feet. Also, this was on his route from feed pit to the milkers' barn and shutting and opening the gates every time was a pain – these cattle were just not thriving in these conditions and Peter held himself to blame every time he passed their door. It was not good enough but there was no room at the inn!

Juggling milk amounts for his contract meant keeping more milking cows and took all the space he had convenient to the milking parlour. Basically he was overstocked and he knew it, but none of these 'extras' came up to scratch for taking to market. It was a Catch 22 situation. He didn't have the nerve to take them to market because they didn't look good enough and he was ashamed to put his farm's name to them, so he put off the inevitable and they spent yet another week in these less than perfect surroundings. As market came round again, Peter went through the same scenario in his head. He knew he was kidding only himself. Admit it Peter, not your best but they just *have to go*.

When Grandmother had been alive there was always the lunchtime discussion of what had happened in the cowshed. Who was needing a new bale and how long this bale had lasted. Very often it was possible to recall which field and even where in a field a certain bale of forage had come from just from the quality and the contents. Some held still yellow flowers, appearing as bright as the pressed flowers his sister used to squeeze between the pages of big books. He always felt these were the 'lucky' bales as if they held sweeties for the cattle, and the more mundane grass-only bales were basic 'dinner', everyday fodder just to keep the quota up. Each bale opening was a thrill to him. He could not remember exactly where the haul had been placed because the contractors had their job to do and whizzed up and down, up and down in their huge machinery tending to the work in double quick time and away, on to the next job, field, harvest, so he lost count of what had come from where. This was his mental jigsaw now, to piece together what he fed daily to his girls. When times moved slower, and he and the family had been in charge of their own harvest, they knew exactly where everything had come from. Had time moved slower then? It seemed like it. They had all baled the hay together and lifted and carried and hauled and sweated together. Were the summers longer? It seemed so. Nowadays it was all about phone calls and arranging and wondering whether your turn would come or whether some bigger fish had priority and the contractor was juggling his own against paid work and the weather. Where exactly was the farming in that? He was, of course, just so grateful to have got his harvest of grass in. A fine long row of black shiny bales. He counted them up and divided by weeks. This would see him through, provided he shifted some of the unnecessary stock. Oh my, with that thought his emotions rose to the surface again. He could no longer put off the inevitable. He went to make another of those phone calls that had become the kind of farming he was forced to do.

It was upon him, he was all booked in, loaded up and off to market. No more treading water. The winter feed calculation had called the last shot. He had to make his fodder stores last until the cattle could go out and eat grass again. An uncertain science since nobody knew what the weather would do the following spring. A cold spring and the grass was slow to grow. A wet spring and the land was too soggy to support the many tromping hooves' twice daily walks from field to parlour. There had to be slack in the system to allow for the vagaries of Nature. This bunch, this motley crew, some large, some small but all just too skinny and not Peter's intended standard at all, they had to go.

Market was excruciating for our man. No one commented to his face, and he saw many 'faces' but he felt it from all sides. Never mind whether it was imagined, it was real enough to Peter. Inwardly he cringed his way through the whole proceeding and although he made reasonable monies, which was a tiny blessing, his pride was very, very hurt. Oh my, not his best day and no wonder he had been avoiding it. But Peter, what you don't realise is that others don't judge you as you judge yourself. What the other farmers had seen was opportunity. Yes, the cattle were a bit skinny, but there was quality in their bones and there lay a profit for those farmers with open barn space and full clamps of feed. Not everyone was struggling with the conundrum of a milking herd, hence the bidding for his cattle had gone better than he thought. It was not enough to alleviate the inner pain of this chap. Poor overworked Peter was so tied up in his own problems he could not see beyond his own prison. The greetings from the market crowd, although returned in like manner, he misconstrued for pity for his bringing these, in his eyes, 'substandard' animals to market. His mind heard only the clamour and clanking of gates, the muffled noise of cows, calves and tractor and lorry engines all rolled into one as his eyes pricked with embarrassment at his changed fortunes. His pride was at rock bottom. No enjoyment was had from being in among his fellow workers, the very people to whom he could be offloading the burden of his problems. The ones who, most likely, would understand at least the mechanics of his problems, if not the emotions. But no, too 'manly', too repressed by upbringing, too overwrought by his own imagined failures to even contemplate a chat.

Head down he hurried through the inevitable paperwork, eyes averted from the secretaries and office bods all doing their jobs, trained to smile and greet with a 'how are you Mister Peter?' not listening or expecting an honest answer and certainly not being given one. The torture of the time queueing to fix the paperwork hurt Peter inwardly and physically he felt sick. Standing in the cosy warmth of an office bustling with humanity, steaming and stinking, suddenly was too much. A sweat broke out on this man's brow, his shirt stuck to his back but he could not remove his jacket. Too warm, but also in need of the security of the familiar. Wrapped in his jacket, his mantle of protection, he stood fearfully, unable to expose himself even down to his shirtsleeves. The time ticked so slowly by. His sale had been successful, he just desired to be away home, back to his own yard among the creatures he knew and loved, wrapped in the familiarity of his routine. Now!

Peter went outside and attended to his evening routine but with a heavy heart. By the time he had returned his mind was made up. He would no longer toe the line, following this trend in farming was killing him on the inside, he may as well take the bull by the horns, give up the farm. Sell up, slow down and bail out before he broke down completely. It felt like that, selling out, he loved farming, the animals, the countryside but not like this, and if it meant he had to get out then to save the last vestiges of his sanity that is exactly what he would do. Sell up, pay off all his debts take a small house on one of the many village estates springing up, sleep for a week. And then what? 'I can worry about that one another day. I'm pooped, I'm out of here.'

Believe in yourself Peter, life is a challenge worth running with until the end. The end for every creature is personal, not dictated by some pencilled in schedule from above, but more to do with getting to the bottom of the list that you came to do. Drag your life out if you will by avoiding the important issues. Important for you is not the same as important for someone else. We can never know or understand anyone else's business. There are some basic moral pointers to regard; common sense used to be a highly rated commodity amongst the populous but it has been replaced by 'evidence based findings'. Who is checking whether the 'evidence' is real or imagined? Strange that our scientists cannot agree. While cars become a similar shape through air tunnel trials, the cars that sell best are rounded and have a character assigned to them. We are not robots, not convinced by evidence if our inner unproven belief is stronger.

Take your evidence and economies of scale and review them in the light of common sense. Yes, it costs much less to put up a barn for 4,000 animals, but common sense says that is way too many, they will get ill. It is an obvious solution to the human housing problem to stack house upon house upon house and make flats. Vertical space comes free, but common sense says: how many people want to live up there? Perhaps there is good reason for balking at the high rise, since it is purported by anthropology that we 'came down from the trees' a long time ago. Sending us upwards, backwards as a species is not the answer. Where would common sense dictate that the forward run of humankind should move? In Peter's world it needs to slow up, just enough for him to catch his breath, to think things through, to release the never ending pressure of more! more! more! for the same rewards. In this world what are the honest and acceptable rewards to be? A safe home – a cosy feel whether you love it alone or tucked into family life? A community spirit where one looks out for another? Enough to feel secure and a reasonable return for a decent day's work? Not much to ask from a civilisation that has been on the go for a few millennia. Have we not worked that one out yet? Duh! Can we even make amends now?

Yes, one by one we can take our own houses in hand, climb off the tall tree of aloofness, be kind to our fellow man as automatically as it is easy to do. Most people are kind, loving in fact. Most people have been a parent and all people have been a child. Common sense says we love our children. When did the love run out? Never. It is hidden in a world of professionalism and getting on up the company ladder, climbing on the heads of the underling to make our own mark. Back off, realise, your turn will come. This life is for experience. Remember, those of you who have read it, The Water Babies and Mrs Doasyouwouldbedoneby? Think it through with common sense. If you mete out that treatment the inevitable will return to you. What goes around, comes around – so beware, stop, change, get wise, work it out. Slow up the world, not to get off, but to cope, kindly, with thought for fellow beings, with fear and trepidation if that is what motivates. Your turn will come. So turn around. Now!

Peter would never be horrible to anyone. His was a gentle nature from the day he was born. His faults lay more in his inability to assert. His wishes to become a farmer, to eschew the further education offered were backed up by Grandmother. Without that strong woman's backing he would have given in, become the pen pusher that he was very able to become. There is nothing wrong with a farmer's brain. He may just choose to run it along a different line from standard education. Farmers have special inner workings, their range is vast and what they cannot at first do themselves they study – Peter would pore over a diagram, a technical manual, a shed design until he had it in three dimensional perfection in his mind. This is what he wanted to chew over with a friend, a fellow worker, discuss the benefits or otherwise of this or that design, talk through modifications he could make to suit his system or to use up leftover materials, recycle those out of use. Modern man Peter, already a natural recycler before it became a catchphrase in the town's world. Our Peter, a man of moderate means, a vast store of knowledge and self-styled ability and gentle with it, only he did not see his intelligence for what it was. Splendid man, we need some more like you Peter.

Chapter 7

A flight in air! A turning point, a tiny hare
spins fortunes for the unaware.

Right on cue, Peter dived under the header to save a leveret from being squashed. His love for the countryside and all the creatures living there was endemic. His was a love borne from connectivity not sentiment. He felt 'at one' with the outdoors life, not fully alive unless reaching out to the horizon on every side. Man had been here before, this land he trod felt trodden before him by other feet. Those feet may have been bound in rags or naked or wearing stout hobnailed boots but whoever and however long ago, they were the feet of mankind and he was part of that race of men who at a different level pushed past the boundaries of their flesh and blood and into the deepest part of their souls where barriers exist not and time exists not. It was from this level the need to save the baby hare came. His need to save a life even whilst putting his own at risk. Luckily for him the giant machine had not fully got up to speed and the driver, a kindly chap, was alert and on the ball. He jammed on his brakes in response to witnessing the unusual action taken by Peter. The lunge toward the header like a rugby tackle, the instinctive foot to the pedal an equal response of humanity for humanity. Stop there – one man instinctively saving a fellow creature, another instinctively saving a fellow man. Stop there, while Peter is headlong in mid-air, arms outstretched towards a leveret, a baby hare. The hare stricken with fear from the deafening roar of the machine above his head and the sight of metal blades descending upon him. Our driver, face contorted in fright at the actions unfolding before him. All of this happening in a split moment in time. Who will come out of this unscathed? Peter? The hare? The driver? Anyone?

Sentiment apart, who do you want to survive this ordeal? Are you on the side of Peter, a man unable to suppress a love of beings, even those apparently lesser than himself? Or do you consider this a rash and stupid action? Or are you with the hare, poor frightened creature unable to move, a giant monster of metal disturbing the home he has made for himself, or been placed in by his loving hare brained parents? Maybe the sympathy is with our driver, a kindly chap, just doing his job. Sent to mow a meadow and confronted with a scene he never dreamt would happen when he got up for work that morning and packed his grub for the day. Which is pulling most at your heartstrings? Well, I leave you there floundering with your feelings for a while longer.

What is the next move for Peter then? Here he is in mid-air, figuratively speaking. He can land with a thump, miss the hare and be eaten up by the machinery or he can hope for another outcome. Which do we allow him to have? Are we influencing Peter in any way at all? One would think that our separate lives flowed along independently, each to their own little stream of being but maybe, possibly, there is another way to look at this. Leave Peter there, safe, as yet unhurt by flailing metal and unfinished in his business with a little creature of the fields.

His growing up, one of common sense and a reverence for all living creatures, of which his grandmother may have placed humans below the reverence bestowed upon animal of the farm and animal of the hedgerows, skies and fields within her ken. She was not a television watcher, therefore had not seen the wonderful images of other regions of our beautiful planet placed in front of her eyes. She may well have been overwhelmed by such sights in any case and certainly she would not understand or condone the cruelty of mankind against this portion of the universe we are privileged to live on. Masters please, of the earth and sky beware the unsightly and unnecessary wrecking of the earth. We all live here, take heed and bring your unbridled passions for havoc under control now.

Back to Peter, do we have any influence on his being? Flying! Can we save him too? Consider his plight like a sad life out of control, in a world desperate to please on the surface, but wrecking the very ground we all depend on every time we take a step. Fair? Maybe not, perhaps it is your job to be in charge of the wrecking ball. Are you? Do you even know or understand the consequences of the actions you take each day? Is this sounding like a lecture? It is.

Peter was brought up to love all creatures. He is not soppy, his is the killing game, producing honest food for your table, an honourable job, one needed by all of us here in our weak and hungry fleshly garments. Would you enjoy a good dinner? Roast meat and potatoes and vegetables, all these can be provided from a farm like Peter's and in addition, milk, cream, yogurt, cheese and butter. Remember also that wheat for bread and barley for beer are also possibilities here on this small farm. Peter cannot do that work on his own, for there is much work to be done in preparing the ground, tilling the soil, feeding the beasts and harvesting their dung to return to the land for the cycle of growth, and returning of goodness. Such an elegant and simple cycle and one that can be carried out by men and women willing to take their exercise in the fields, feel the wind and rain on their faces and return to a table of good grub for a lunch.

How idyllic this sounds. No it is not idyllic, it is the natural order of life which has been driven from its destined path and been skewed by greed. Who wishes for all the profits from Peter's farm? For Peter gets few, sometimes nothing for the work he does. He cannot sustain this. It is akin to asking him to sustain flying in the air for longer than the natural laws of gravity and momentum will allow. Who are these magicians who conspire away from Peter's farm and drag his money to their already bursting bellies? Willing him to carry out an act of total selflessness in the caring for his animals, to their advantage. Who are they? Who are you?

Understand that in the idyllic scenario, Peter shares his farm. It may, by dint of birth, be his to organise and make order from, but he will willingly share. Come work with Peter for a day. Arrive from nearby in your car, or better still awake on the farm, sharing some lodgings with fellow workers. Enjoy a breakfast together of bread, made from the grains grown here on the farm, milled in the house and cooked in a range fired from wood garnered from those hedgerows that fence around the fields. Strong compounds for animals, trimmed by hand of man and the browsing act of animal mouths, each branch, twig and leaf with its own place in this natural world, a different shape, a different taste and a different range of interesting gifts to balance the hay and silage grown in the fields. The fields taking turns to grow the feed for cattle, sheep and fowl. Mankind tending to a garden, tilled for many generations and soft and fluffy earth bolstered by excellent composts, loved and tended. The heat from the compost allowing an extended season of growth to alleviate the boredom of cabbage again! But round the table, camaraderie, comfort from loneliness. Stories and Life where 'cabbage again' can be tolerated and even loved, for when the seasons turn and change, there is celebration in the first beans, strawberries and joy of joy – sweetness. This is where our farms should be, and horticulture, not used only as a therapy but as a living. Come those of you who yearn to escape the tiredness of city life and commute, gird up your loins and become the people who understand fruitfulness. Be there, underneath Peter, ready to catch him and his natural world, before those mock magicians expect Peter to perform unnatural acts of balance and airborne acrobatics so they can whip the ground from under his feet and the money from his coffers. They have not yet the sense to understand it is also their own world they are ruining, such are the blinkers of their greed.

It is six in the morning the day after the mower/hare/driver incident. Peter is not in bed, he has been up for hours and worked his way through the morning slog of cows and udders and milk and wash down and cows again. He has fed the calves and stripped down a tractor needing an oil and water freshen up. All in all he has probably done more than most manage in a whole day. He survived the headlong leap, otherwise our story may now be taking a different turn. The driver survived his heart-stopping moment and the little hare, given that extra few seconds for his inborn instincts to kick in gathered his courage and scarpered, gone, quick as a flash.

We have all had those moments when instinct overtakes, a hand grabbed back from a burning flame, the dive onto the footbrake on cue as someone unwittingly steps off a pavement in front of us. A lunge towards a toppling toddler – how many have experienced the 'wide' zone around a newborn's head – ultra awareness heightening our senses just for a while? Tucked inside these feeble bodies is something else, abilities that surface instantly when called upon by danger, protectiveness, love for a fellow being. All these three felt something out of the ordinary just for a while. Peter, his unquestioning desire to save but, without the layering in of the driver's instinct tied to his training, flowing immediately into the well-executed emergency stop, it could have been disaster for both Peter and the hare. The driver would then have had the trauma of an accident, hardly looked at the hare and been taken up in shock at what he might have dealt with but that is not what happened.

Go back. Peter headlong in mid-air, driver, face contorted, leg slamming into motion. Peter scoops up the tiny creature and arises triumphant from under the now stilling blades, his face gleaming with success. The driver relaxes, automatic hands switching off the engine and is down out of the cab in a flash. The incident forgotten, all eyes on the baby hare. Look! look! says the expression on Peter's face.

I see! I see! in the answering expression from the driver. There is no admonishment, no harsh words spoken. The leveret is the centre of attention, his big fearful eyes, oversized ears flat against his back, short front legs and lanky long hind springers. Both big grown men melted by the helplessness of this creature's situation. His scrape, his hollow, home to a baby, now exposed. Where will he go now? Obviously still young enough to need parental support, the conversation of the men turned to what should happen next. One in favour of a complete saviour situation, into taking the poor dear thing home, feeding it milk from a dropper. Total intervention and removal from its natural environment. The other, the original saviour looking from a different perspective seeing the merit in damage limitation, finding a solution closer to home. Leaving the course of nature to run unaided further by mankind. Letting the little hare go here within his own environment, no more disturbances for the day. Let them finish now for the evening and hope that parent hares find the young offspring and tend to his needs. And what will those needs be for a tiny creature? Placed gently onto the ground, our hare at last in charge of his faculties. The lanky hind legs pushing off, in double time he sped away. No more noise from the engine and an hour or two of peaceful evening brought the wild creatures together as a family again, a feed from mother and a sleep beside her body warmth sufficed to blot out the terrors of the day, possibly a little wiser, understanding the need to run from approaching engine noise. This little hare may live to adulthood himself.

All the while, in our atomic world, the greater extent of the goo, that atomic cluster replication and splitting was carrying on, joining and dividing in equal measure but soon to be disturbed as Peter's cleansing programme, another part of his daily routine, clicked into place. The regular cleansings were his to perform, the dangers of non-compliance too awful to contemplate, inspections and fines hung over his head and Peter was desperate for normal movements to be allowed again. Even to be able to welcome the postman onto his yard would be a treat, a joy even.

Our telescopic vision perfected, take a glimpse into this world again. Unwitting but somehow in touch with the evolutionary process of change for the better, one little atom being, grabbed the chance for change, instead of the ever smooth replicating transaction force for force, he strained at another level – made something happen, changed himself forever. How? We cannot tell, we cannot enter the consciousness of such a tiny thing but it happens, mutations happen and our little fellow mutated. Spinning with the excitement of difference he no longer formed the exact pattern of his 'before' life and was pushed upwards, outwards from the goo. Alone, still befuddled by the change in circumstance, moved and shunted out of the general sweep of direction. In all senses our chap took another direction and this happened on Peter's farm.

This tiny atom, barely a width apart from his mates has passed the point of no return in his mutation. It is a fact of life that mutations take place as Life strives for another experimental form of itself and here this little being had done it, become a Little Mutation. His new unique shape, his difference aided by the blasting force of Peter's washings, squeezed him beyond the reach of the disinfectant's clutches and left him, one on his own in a strange world. Strange world indeed. Where the disinfectant had been applied was now well washed down by Peter who did not like to leave the goo, even once dead, in case any of it was still volatile. Little did he know that his treatment had been thorough on the one hand and yet at the same time had helped create a substance new to the world. The shape of the Little Mutation allowed it to escape the burning clutches of the fierce disinfecting chemicals and now breathing, in his own manner, the little atom rested up, allowed the wash of Peter's hose to carry him along, deposit him, unaware of his next role in life. No one, nothing is aware at that small level, or is it?

Peter's body had been affected by his moods, his disappointments and now small triumph. He had saved the hare, triumphed in the face of a death or mutilation unthinkable. This small act, its positive outcome, showed in his demeanour and his demeanour was held up by a structure of atoms. Atoms made his bones and flesh and blood and these carried the Peter we now know to be the gentle soul he is – can we therefore also conclude that this small and singular mutation of an atom, our Little Mutation, similar and yet not the same as his previous self, is also in some way self-aware? Dare we make such an assumption? We can see him, through our imagination microscope washed up at the edge of the ditch, untouchable by disinfectant, not dead, not wrecked or pulled apart like the other atoms of goo had been, not rendered lifeless and due to be dust himself, but the opposite, ready to carry out yet another transformation. He was on a roll, having achieved this tiny shape shift that allowed Life to continue, where for his previous fellow atoms it had not. He was ready, strong from straining for the new. He did it again, strained in experimental glee to find out what can possibly be around the corner, figuratively speaking. Here was a new growth, a new life. Does he now just need the roll of the dice to be in his favour several times over to become a new species? Or does this small being, come into being, dragged through by the positive mood on Peter's farm now? Is it a time capsule for Peter's future life, one that he does not even know himself to be or have? Is Peter shifting the atmosphere on his farm so much with the positivity of his tiny triumph that not only his demeanour but also his surroundings are changing, starting with this one tiny life of being, this little shifting speck graciously attenuating and moulding itself to its surroundings but in response to what?

Chapter 8

Night terrors reign, darkness descends with thoughts of madness and brutal ends.

Coming under the heading of terrible, a terror descended upon Peter in the night. His bedclothes were already soaked in sweat by the time he managed to wrest himself from his inner turmoil. Who had been calling him in his dream? Where was the familiarity from? He swam around in his head searching for elucidation. One minute he had been asleep, unconscious to the world and then, writhing in some snake-like thrashing entity, part of the flailing limbs but not actually in control. The monster of his dreams wore him like an accessory, chucked, tossed over one shoulder but ready to be cast aside should something better, more stylish, more stunning, 'smarter', come along. And even though he felt joined to this monster he also felt reticent as if the feeding arteries were fraily joined and might snap and shrivel, dropping him like a cast off autumn leaf to blow in the wind, later to be caught up in some gutter and turn to anaerobic slop, stinking and cloying, hoping vainly for some active part in Life but knowing his place was deadened, inactive, apart from the feeding bacteria breaking him down into the inevitable dust.

This awful feeling of helplessness was upon him when he woke. His bedclothes in disarray evidenced his uneasy rest. Time after time he made the effort to piece together what it was that had so upset him. Normally he slept well enough, fatigued from his daily labours, and although worries were often upon him they more frequently attacked his waking rather than sleeping hours. This was different. The quality of the disturbance much realer than a dream, there was a record within him of the rubbery feel of the monster limbs, or were they tentacles? Maybe there were no words to describe but just remembrances of the panicked feeling of being caught up in something much bigger than he can manage. So big he was hardly acknowledged yet he was also necessary for this monster to live, to suck juices, claim a living from other frail bodies. The monster was disparate, difficult to pin down, real and yet like a blob of mercury, elusive, possibly as poisonous, but certainly not as beautiful. Come face to face with any part of it and it presented a gleaming smile, impossible to get behind, scary, disturbing, soul-suckingly terrifying. No wonder he was sweating. And now he was cold.

Had he created this monster himself? No, it was too large for him to have created by himself – where was its energy and life coming from? Now fully awake, he sensed a childlike memory of bad fairies and trolls and ogres from the storybooks of his youth. Grimms' Fairy Tales had held him in fascinated awe as a child, hardly daring to read the stories, immersed, believing. The Arabian Nights, again Bluebeard loomed out of the recesses of his mind, the silhouette pictures of slain queens lined up in a chamber sent a shiver down his spine. His experience, for he could not call it a dream, it held more substance than that, spoke to him wordlessly, warning him of the fragility of his situation. He recognised himself as a part of the monster, feeding and being fed upon yet not controlling it and it felt terrible.

Here we have Peter, at his wits' end, so close to a deed that under different circumstances he would never countenance, but this forcing, pushing him to the brink has been under the very eyes of those advising him, expecting him to be able to perform miracles of sustained effort, day after painful day. Barely being able to cover costs, far less look to the gradually dwindling strength of the ancient tumbling buildings of a farm he used to be so proud to be able to call his home. All had become worrisome, and now tiresome, his temper was no longer equal. Peter is not a hot-headed man, nor lazy, but a new task added into his overloaded mind sent him into inward huffing and puffing, and internal lectures given to imaginary clerks in imaginary offices in imaginary buildings remote, citied or countried far off. His was a remote life, but the lives of those who held him as a puppet on their strings seemed remote and ridiculous to him. He imagined besuited officials sitting round committee tables, being very serious about subjects they had never had the pleasure or *displeasure* of doing. Demanding and debating with each other about the ins and outs, costs and benefits of schemes that would no longer touch their lives once the decisions were made and they were onto the next item on their agenda. Their decisions would rock Peter's boat again and again, give him extra tasks to fit in around a routine that already filled his days and emptied his bank account. He huffed at their ability to sit and rake in his money, his taxes going to fund this ridiculous situation he found himself in – he paid them to make rules for him to carry out to the letter of their law, or be fined, punished, even banned for transgressing, but if he were not there they would have no one to make rules for and then, what on earth would the likes of the self-asserted cerebral types even do?

Questions such as this rotated in his head, spun round with the unfairness of it all. He could not even take time away from the roundabout of his life to protest, explain the nonsense, try to make anyone see sense; all this added to his sense of helplessness. His rules would be that nobody in a decision-making position should get there only because they could pass exams, they had also to have lived it fully to the core. Look back, he thought, to the days of BSE, bovine spongiform encephalitis if you like the big words, they would! Whoever in their right mind thought that feeding meat protein to a cow was a good idea? Madness, yes, madness literally was what comes of spoiling the natural order too much, and that was too much. That you can dupe a cow into eating sweeties with powdered meat crystals in it isn't difficult, after all, people have been sneaking poison into each other's food for years, but if the clever scientist in his ivory tower had been someone who had worked with cows, really worked with cows and knew their nature through and through they would have known, these gentle creatures are vegetarian. Sneak what and where you like but the true knowledge was there for anyone with a heart to absolutely know – 'NO MEAT thank you, I am a cow'. Obvious common sense, and anyway, why? Greedy, a different kind of warped half-cocked idea of sense again. Give more protein, concentrated protein and more protein-heavy milk comes out. No! More stress comes out from that kind of science. Send that person, the one who started that idea, back to the byre, to mooch in the shed with the cows, to understand their nature and they would know, just like Peter knows that all this pushing cannot come to any long term good.

He just does not have the energy to pay attention anymore. How can he get out, slide out from under the weight of these false reasonings put before him, before the last resort is the one he opts for? No, Peter, please do not even think it. You are too good at solving practical problems Peter. Do not think up the mechanics of that one, for you will make it work and we need you for this story, this allegory of life and work and fragmented living. We need you Peter to piece yourself back together, to take that madness out of your life, for if you carry out that last action – you will be considered mad; if you fail in that, what you consider to be your last job ever, then you will be doled out time with a psychiatrist. Take the madness out of your life, you have been pushed

Peter, right to your brink. Draw back, lean on one of your cow's backs, she will do her best to support you Peter, her race has been here too – been proffered the poison apple. She told you from within that she would never eat the poison unless it was so hidden she could not distinguish it from what was meant to be good fodder.

Peter, recognise now that these subsidies that are being fed to you, offered as sweeties to lure you beyond your natural capabilities, will push you beyond your brink – into madness too. Shun the sweeties, the apple laced with poison. You have taken one bite, and the griping pains are already upon you. Resist now, and allow the cleansing healing of what your mind, your own intelligence can bring to the surface for you to regenerate. Push out the poison Peter, you may well vomit, eject and reject that which is a false grasping for you to produce more than is humanly possible. Just as your cows were forced to produce more than is cow-ly possible. Help Peter, help Peter, support him like his cow is now. She holds this man, barely able to stand on his own feet. This cow, for he has gone to her for what solace he can glean in his state of wretchedness, his girl, Number 476 is there, even now, although she has seen grief. She will support you Peter. Can we support Peter? Can we be there under him and catch him and soothe him and say, 'Yes Peter – I will buy your goods, I must eat and I shall choose my food from your farm to keep you afloat, alive and in good health. My good work will support your good work.'

Let us come together, put back the fragments of our broken society with small steps of union, of helping hands and fair exchange.

'Pint of milk, Madam?'

'Yes, but only for a fair price.'

Peter was through the worst of his bad times, him not realising it yet, but this will come, and perhaps there is another surprise up ahead that would have been forgone without these tricks of timing that life plays on all of us.

Who is to say that our difficult moments are not our finest moments? For if we can cope with them, see our way through them as best we can, then is that possibly what this life journey is for? Hard hitting I know, but always there in the back of the mind is the age old question on the philosopher's lips. Who am I? Where do I come from and where do I go? There are answers, but they are personal. They are borne of experience alone and the dragging along the bottom, of a life trying to be lived well, may be exactly the place to slough off the old skin of worn out ideas, given, not earned. The place to shed old habitual thoughts, believed and not challenged. Without the stress and strain of pain would changes ever be made? Would we strive to new ideals, dare to make the future bright again by looking with a new light, from a different angle? Poised as Peter was to bail out, give up, maybe in a very permanent manner, could he then have gained anything from the suffering he experienced? Better to see it through, strive to change, look for a way forward. Ask for help, yes, ask for help. Ask for help and recognise it when it is given. Hang on Peter, change is happening around you.

Revisit the pain of the atom, straining in the gutter to make a similar kind of change that Peter now has to make to improve his lot. Peter must change his environment to move on; the atom must change himself in order to survive in the environment he finds himself. Carried along with the whoosh of a hosepipe, swirling downwards into a ditch, this small being has escaped the burning intensity of chemical warfare and his efforts have toughened him in such a way as to encourage the change. He has slipped the death he so nearly had and is resting up, but a surprise is round the corner here too, the joining of forces to make something new. Peter will also join forces one day but that is for the future of our story. Meanwhile, Peter's struggle was mental, his breakthrough one of mental strength and he will forever keep that strength.

How can we equate the struggle this atom has experienced? What change allowed his escape? Did he make that effort himself? Was the life force in him stronger than in his fellow atoms, allowing his extra push of determination to carry out the transformation that made the difference? What force was it that mutated this one above all others? Chance or desire for change? Did the mediocre succumb and the unique survive? Is this a fair comparison? Is the strength that Peter showed, to pull through when he was so very nearly willing to give up, his unique gift? For he could no longer run with the pack, be hounded along by the conventional flow towards more cows, larger quantities, false economies of scale that outgrew his small farm's capabilities. Is it fair to say that he is in this special order of unique, taking back his power, putting his ideas into action, looking again at his strengths and those of his unique situation? Releasing the old news of 'everything must get bigger', for what it was – somebody else's idea. The somebody there on the edge of farming, calling the shots and stripping the profits before any meaningful return can filter down to where it belongs, with the worker, the farmer and therefore the cows. For if the situation had been different and there was a fair return on the many hours of labour that Peter put in he would have made it work. Peter is no slacker.

Remember the other tiny atom we assigned a fellowship to at the beginning of the story? Here is a reminder. This little fellow makes up the outer world you experience, you stand on him, and use him for breath and food. At night you lay your body made from pieces of him onto a bed made from other pieces of the very same stuff. Different combinations and in different states of wet, dry or airy float around you, support you when you swim and challenge you up mountain and down valley. This whole world is made of those tiny, tiny pieces jig-sawed together so cleverly, so seamlessly that you take it all for granted. Take a little piece of this stuff and come closer once again. Enter the spell that is the internal of an atom but never forget that your world is made from this. Undeniably now you touch, smell and feel it with its self-same stuff. Are we getting close? Is it freaking you out to come to such a realisation? Do you need to step back, just to reassess, make sure that the world as you generally know it is still there for you? Phew it is! Reassured, approach again, draw in very close and let me guide you to the place where the solutions are. They reside within, and your route within can be chosen by you, for now we use this one. Put your eye close to the eyepiece of your imagination telescope, seek out the inner world of a tiny atom, swirl with it just a second until you readjust to this other world, other kind of space, a counter space to the one you everyday inhabit, a hugeness residing within a smallness and every atom has this possibility. The scale of the world turned inside out, no longer measureable with tape or timing device, nevertheless as real as anything else in this world. This world expands to accommodate your needs. Let Peter also seek his way through his problems to a new inner world where he may be able to find some peace, so we follow him further.

Chapter 9

A voice of calm breaks through the racket putting Peter back on track. It opens avenues anew and broadens Peter's inner view.

A crashing bore, not the sort of expression Peter would normally use but this time he meant it. The crashing part came from the awful noise in his head. Ever since he could remember he had been able to listen inside his head. As a child it had been part of his going to sleep routine, he loved it. When he had been read a bedtime story he could then go into the store in his head and relive the story but this time with landscapes and characters coming to life. His had been a rather strange growing up. On the farm there had been the fun and routine of the animals, the security of family life going on all about him, but also for him a sense that somehow he was different. This difference was not something outwardly showing. He was a charming young man, clever and courteous but still just a little strange, unique. There was a kind of fearlessness in his demeanour, imperceptible to the average onlooker but commented on by family members who knew him well. His grandmother lived with the family for as long as he could remember. It was very common in those days; Grandmother had a downstairs room that smelled exactly like her. Now it had become a general dumping ground full of little used suitcases and 'good' winter clothes left over from the days of woollen herringbone tweed jackets. That room probably had 'the moth'. My! Grandmother would be spinning in her grave. But Peter didn't have time for mothproofing, he was on another mission altogether.

This crashing bore was annoying him intensely, the racket in his head, classed as tinnitus by his doctor, was getting worse. It started about the time *the incident* happened, or so he thought, so difficult to pinpoint. It wasn't bad at first, just a background thin sort of noise. If he listened out for it, or rather when he noticed it, he could focus his attention on it but had no control. It was neither rhythmic nor regular but came in random bursts of the same frequency. Hmmmmmmmm mmm mmmmmmmm mmm mmmmmmm mmmmmm m m mmmmm mm. On and on, then the next time he thought about it, it was gone, only to return as a surprise. The only regular thing he could say was that he noticed it most frequently when he was in bed. He used to be able to forget about it in the day, too busy and outside noises covered it anyway. It had, however, lately, been there night and day and was getting worse, covering more frequencies and in general becoming a crashing bore.

As he lay in bed, absentmindedly listening into his headspace racket, a thought came to him. He remembered how he had 'been in charge' of this internal world in his head as a child and wondered whether he could similarly fill up the space with his own racket and drown out this annoyance. No harm in trying he supposed. But how? Wracking his brains he remembered snatches from some of the stories of his youth. It was the three dimensional world of play in his head that was realer than the words on the page that had been read to him. He remembered himself dressed as one of the characters in Peter Pan, not the main man – the Peter in that story was far too important for him to play – but he was one of the Lost Boys, happy under the protection of his main man. Funnily enough, putting this fleshed up remembrance in the way of the crashing bore noise worked. He had reprieve for just a while and had the added bonus of reliving what had been for him a good fun time of his life, pre big responsibilities and when he was surrounded by a supporting extended family too. The memory faded and the crashing bore returned. Oh well, resigned to it, he did his best to ignore it and turned over to go to sleep. The only other time when he was not being internally harangued.

'Please stop the racket,' said Peter within his mind. We all take this turn from time to time, we all give ourselves a little talking to. Perhaps a pep talk when a new or difficult situation arises, a reminder to ourselves to take a deep breath before jumping into a complicated situation, but do you expect an answer? Peter got an answer. Right then a return voice spoke to him.

'What do you mean stop the racket? Peter, this is what you ordered up.'

The shock within Peter sent a jolt through him. It was such a real voice, not his own voice surely? He was still trying to work out whether he had heard it with inner or outer ears when it came about again.

'If we stop the racket what will you replace it with?'

Peter was too dumbstruck to answer, to think even. He had heard of people hearing voices, but thought it was some sort of symptom of madness. A quick flutter of fear thrilled through him. Was he going mad? The Voice came again, a slight impatience to it.

'Well are you going to answer? What will you fill the space with when the racket is removed?'

Recovering his internal voice Peter gave a lame, 'I don't know'.

The Voice, this time appearing to be sporting a body, not so much a body that Peter could see, but he sensed it. This was a being of sorts, not a voice hanging in space. Space had coalesced round The Voice and become very interesting to Peter, he was drawn in by its presence, its feeling of certainty as if there was an important truth to be learnt here. He didn't know what he would replace the annoyance of this tinnitus with. It never used to be an issue having to decide what he would like or not like in his head space. Puzzled, he reassessed this 'head space' and came up with the obvious solution. They were thoughts, usually they just got on with themselves, muddled about the place, flitted over one or other of his worries, perhaps hopes, or looked back over a part of the day, week, year. They worried about the weather. Yes, they worried a lot about the weather and how that would affect his farming year. His thoughts, were they talking back? It was apparent that whatever, or whoever this was could tell exactly what was going on within him. That was a bit of a shock. Here he was in his own bed, alone with his thoughts, or so he would have told anyone else and Crash, Bang Wallop – no he was not. What to do now?

Peter was naturally a polite and gentle man so he acted as he would to any stranger. He greeted him and asked what he was supposed to do? The Voice asked him how he thought he had managed to create the situation where his thoughts had turned to a roaring noise. What was he drowning out? The thoughts in his head reeled. With the tinnitus removed for this time, as if rolled back like a carpet being removed for a dance, the imprints of the past hectic dance of his life were revealed. Scuffs and dents and a criss-cross of conflicting marks corresponded to his troubled times. No pattern, no order except a faint daily routine marked out in vague prints. Feet walking the same path daily but trailing a despondent chiffon-like waft of indecision, unsettled fears. This is how his life was shown, revealed in those strange moments before the rug rerolled itself, shutting out the brief vision and settling back to the now tiring but familiar chunder and hum in his head. At last he slept.

The following morning he had, at first, forgotten all about the strange experience. There was a flimsy thought that he needed to remember something, but exactly what eluded him. Slowly, over the next couple of hours whilst attending to his automatic daily routine, a remembrance of The Voice came back. He wondered at it. It was a difficult thing to pin down exactly but there appeared to be much truth in it. Yes, he was trying to drown several things out in his life. The unhappiness of the situation he had just accepted. The dislike of the tasks put his way. Financially he had felt he was sliding in an ever backwards manner and he could not envision a way out. Were all these things what he was drowning out with that interminable racket in his head? It was so tiring. AHHHHHHHHHHHHHHHHHHH! The penny dropped in Peter's thoughts. He was alone on the farm and feeling overwhelmed by his situation. No money, no companion and even his stock did not cheer him with their looks – dull and shady outlines is the way he viewed them through tearful eyes. My God, please let this come to an end one way or the other, I am crippled inside with fear for the future when all I should be doing is being grateful that I have a roof over my head and a job I profess to love but that I cannot make come right round about me. *Help me please someone.* This internal wrangling was going on inside Peter's head; even a trip to visit Margaret had not cleared the air for him this time.

He was stumped, what to do next?

This was the morning after The Voice broke through his tinnitus. The noise in his head added to his angst and confusion and the breakthrough had been a relief, but one that he had stored under the category of dream since he had nowhere else in the filing cabinet of his brain to stash it. But it had not been a dream, and with those pleading words The Voice was back and with it a calm space in his head and a faint reminder of the scene under the carpet where his life's footsteps were revealed as a scurrying uncontrolled mess of scuffs and skids in the dust of his life so far.

'Take control Peter, before you do something irreversible.'

What was this penny? And where did it drop into? The slot in Peter's mind, previously hidden from view, for he could not dare to admit his feeling to himself. He was terrified of the thoughts that had closed in, terrified to admit them and also terrified that he may rashly do something. Peter was not a hot-headed man but he was a man of action practical and well able to put in place a scheme that would work. He was wrestling with himself not to allow this practical side of his mind to think the unthinkable. He was not ready to go anywhere but

131

up. The only problem being that he could not think himself out of this ghastly mood that held him flat at the bottom of his capabilities. No amount of internal pep talks and admonishments made any difference, like an addict talking himself out of the next drink and simultaneously opening the bottle, his black mood held him firmly.

The Voice, unspeaking but with clarity, led his thoughts in another direction. Strange feelings swam in front of him. He felt rebirthed in that moment, something like he imagined a snake must feel when his tight and dry, too small skin finally sloughs off and leaves the new silky feeling of perfect fit with room to grow into. Suddenly he felt as if he did have something to look forward to, why? Nothing had changed in that moment at an outer level but inwardly a shift had taken place and the terrifying thoughts melted. Common sense opened out in front of him as if a new path had been swept into view. Peter took his life – in his hands – but this time in a positive manner, so close had he been to taking his life permanently. The end of a road, or the beginning?

Peter's determination kicked in first, just managing to squeeze between the despair and despondency of the situation and the tiny glimmer of hope that Peter always held close to his heart. He would jolly well take things in hand himself. The banks would just have to wait a few days and he would take this particular bull by the horns. He had the deeds for the farm, Grandmother had these stored in her paperwork, there was no will that he had seen. He made an appointment at the local solicitors and, deeds in hand, went for a free half hour talk. Peter had made a comprehensive list of what he needed to understand, he must at least clear the doubts he had about the farm ownership and was determined not to waste any of this precious time. No way would he be paying solicitor fees unless something very different happened in his life. The interview went something like this. Peter showed his list straight away to the junior solicitor who scanned it over and then looked up on his computer. Big surprise, a reference to Grandmother's will. No one had thought to ask a solicitor. The presumption being that Grandmother would have such an important document alongside all her other papers.

Everything changed. The will was found and the interview took a totally different turn. This will made Peter the sole inheritor of the farm as long as he was actively farming, and he could make all decisions in that light to keep the farm active. Should he, however, wish to give up the activity of farming then the revenue from the sale of the farm would be divided amongst her grandchildren. These were the strangers that Peter had met at Grandmother's wake and he had not warmed to them then. Huh – an easy decision then, he would keep on farming and he would, now he understood his position, be able to contemplate shrinking the farmland to release some funds since he was in charge.

With a huge sense of relief, Peter wondered why nobody had thought to go down that route in search of a will, but life had infilled in its usual way and once the funeral was over, people went back to their own business.

This is a great piece of news, thinks Peter. He has the documents in front of him stating his complete autonomy with the farm as long as he is actively farming it. Grandmother had been an astute businesswoman in her day and improved the farm alongside others of her time but she could see the forward trend and knew Peter would struggle. She also knew that Peter's heart was in this farm and he would do all he could to keep it going. The only omission she had made was to inform anyone of her wishes. It might have saved a lot of heartache if Peter had known this earlier. He could have made clear to the vultures who appeared at Grandmother's funeral that there was no legacy for them while he used this dear farm for its intended purpose. Or was there a higher order of plan here in place? Do we ever know? Can we ever tell?

Peter got in touch with his sister, the only member of his family left to confide in, and asked her to visit. He had something important to tell her and he needed to do this face to face. Meanwhile, the impatient banks would have to wait, he would soon be in the clear and his head was spinning with new plans and decisions. Peter was lifted just a little from his pit of despair and he muttered a prayer of thanks to Grandmother for putting this in place for him. Now he had to keep farming and he owned a farm, what a turnaround of events in such a short time. Life is full of surprises, some good and some more difficult to deal with.

Today was one of trepidation for our man, Peter, had to go through with something he had been dreading. It hadn't used to feature at all on his radar but recently with all the internal commotion and his desperate feelings he knew he must tackle this situation or crumple in a heap, and since that was never going to be an option, it was time to get on with it, his sister's visit. He needed time alone with her around that staple of all discussion, a cup of tea. Peter explained his position on the farm and how financially he was no longer able to grow the business in the manner needed to keep up with the current trend for expansion at all cost, especially since the financial returns were barely a shaving more than the outgoings. He could no longer join with the schemes of others and told her that he had made his mind up. He would go independent, or sell, he was just warning her of potential changes to come, and to ask her blessing.

His sister was well catered for in her off the farm life and had in reality severed any emotional connection with her growing up place. This family was a kindly one and she gave Peter permission to do as he pleased, she would not be hanging over his shoulder like some harpy waiting to tear a piece of his flesh. Peter was so relieved. She didn't offer to help in any practical manner but the emotional relief was enormous and soon spurred Peter on to seeing his way through the paperwork. Grandmother had protected Peter's right to live on the farm as long as he farmed, without conditions. Thank you Grandmother, she knew just how much the farming lifestyle was entwined with Peter's whole psyche.

With this looming uncertainty off his mind Peter felt he could see a glimmer of hope and moved lighter on his feet for it. Gratitude flooded from him as he walked the farm. He thanked his sister for being true to her upbringing and remaining the generous person that was the child he had grown up with. He thanked Grandmother for protecting his first love – farming – and most of all he thanked with gratitude this wonderful piece of ground and the animals he was sanctioned with caring for.

Peter peered with renewed interest into the hedges as he tended to his daily rounds. He knew where the blackbirds nested and the owls hung out in the evening gloom. He farmed to allow them to live alongside him, recognising the need for rough as well as smooth land. He was as keen to harvest the joy of birdsong in his heart as he was milk in the pail. The trees' outlines were to him the rugged forehead of the man he called Farm. For Peter it was wordless but so much on this farm was wordless. Wordless because it was so much bigger than words can even convey. How does the sight of Nature changing imperceptibly slowly in front of your eyes translate into anything but poetry? The harshness of the weather as much a facet of this farming jewel as the tiny robin perched in the tree top singing his loud,

loud heart out when the roaring wind should drown it out and yet he continues singing his song of joy and fierce attachment to this place.

Such was Peter's heart, lighting up from this revelation that, by law, he could stay. He had been given reprieve from having to move, his place was here as long as he could make it work for himself and that was a good feeling. Gone were the jagged thoughts of separation, of inevitable gloom in packing up, gone were the involuntary scenes played out in his mind of cows off to market, farm sales and despondency. Now all he had to do was to find a way to make it work for himself. The light shone from him and every part of his farm felt it at that self-same moment, for Peter and his farm were One.

Chapter 10

*Up or down, out or in? A secret place
revealed within.*

It is on this day, one year ago that Peter was asking himself just this question. Where do I go from here? Somehow he had fallen out with his advisors, not seen eye to eye with their plans for his farm. After all it was his farm, handed down to him through the family. Once upon a time his family had made an adequate living here, brought up their children, paid their way in life. OK, hard work and not much in the way of luxuries; holidays and the likes, but they had not noticed that. All this buzzing about all over the world on holidays didn't appeal to Peter anyway. His own cosy bed, surrounded by the animals and people he loved was worth all the beer in Magaluf, or Ibiza or any of the common haunts of the guys down at the local pub. No thank you, quaff your chips and beer in this country. If it is a foreign holiday you crave then go local and experience the true values of the place. He loved his work, he loved his animals, he just could no longer cope with the pressures on him and the daft demands that, on paper looked reasonable, but in real life just made things difficult, so he had changed things.

Today the shift in consciousness came to him. Unusually he was awake before the alarm clock. 'I think I have at last caught up with my sleep' Peter thought to himself. Having had many months of stress, reliving old horrors and fighting off the urge to give up completely, this day was the turnaround day. Like the silent point of a fulcrum, the magical place where the weight from one direction changes to the weight of an opposite direction, the no place, the strangest point in the universe where the nothingness hangs and cannot hang, that tiny, tiny, cannot-put-your-finger on it point of which there are millions upon millions surrounding us in our daily lives. The midpoint of a child's seesaw, the place where the twist of a coin can open the most solidly stuck lid of a shoe polish tin. The point where a screwdriver shoved under suddenly shifts something that has been jammed, glued on with the dirt and rust of ages, the long end of the spanner turning against a bolt. Resting, but cannot be rested on, the no-point or the more miniscule than miniscule, less than microscopic place, yet no-place, where that magical turning point is reached.

How can it be touched upon? Measure it and it

can only be one thing or the other, up or down? Stuck or freed? Still or in motion, the lever, the enormous strength of the lever, where does it reside? Somehow it is beyond the ordinariness of everyday life, rests here in our space but also in another kind of space, and the other kind of space is where Peter was resting right now. He had not yet moved forward in his consciousness to have made a change, yet he was also not the Peter we, or he, had known. This Peter was teetering, not on an edge but in a middle. Teetering right there at the fulcrum point where the strength of his universe was most potent and this gave the idea of his potential. Great things would come of this moment, this balance neither in his old camp of thoughts, where he had felt sorry for himself, sorry for his old deeds and in general sorry mess of life. His potential started right now by moving from this ultimate point of balance, the indescribable place where change takes place. But did he actually desire to take that next step? Here was our Peter, a man of middle years, experience under his belt. A man with a set of values that had grown out of the life he had led, the education and nurturing he had lived through, just getting along the very best he could in the scheme of things, what would or even could change? This was not a place of thought, for thought required some kind of effort. This was a place for gifts, packages of ideas to be slipped through this infinitesimal gap between one side's movement and the other. A gap so slight that it is totally missable in the hustle and bustle of everyday living. A gap so slight yet so powerfully full of ideas when it is touched upon.

Here was Peter, neither up nor down, no longer stuck but not yet moving, here in this place the strength of the universe was upon him. He did not know that, in this position he did not *know* anything. The boot was on the other foot. The *knowing* was upon him. How could that be? Our Peter had not planned his future out, it was more that he was determined to leave behind the uncomfortable workload, the distasteful manner in which he had been forced gradually to treat his fellow beings, his animals, who had been treated as friends and companions in his youth. This relationship had been eroded, moved towards a relationship based around economies of scale, of what was financially viable regardless of what suited Peter's sensibilities. Peter did not have a firm plan to move forward into, just a recoiling horror to move away from. That was what had led him to this position. The difficult legal situation, at first unclear and therefore looming like a vague but ghastly illusion had been reeled in, torn apart to reveal a doable solution. What had appeared too difficult to mention on the obligatory family high day and holiday visits was broached, broken into and dealt with, and a once never thought of plan, selling off a portion of the farm, all completed done, signed and sealed. Hooray, the farm was his, at least what was left of it and he would make the best of it. Less land, therefore fewer cows meant less work, fewer overheads. Yes, less income but that was something to work on, he had a cushion to lean on just now.

His situation was very different now; he had removed himself from the government-led schemes. From that point of view the timing had been good. The advisors were busy cooking up another plan for him that would tie him into more subsidies for years to come, but the downside was the workload. These people came for one day and thought they understood the business. That may be true for some farms but sure as hell, they did not understand Peter. Inwardly, this man had been tired, drained, fed up and on the verge of a nervous breakdown. It was not the physical work, he did enough for two men. It was the heartbreak, the feelings of despondency that washed over him, guilt. His guilt felt the same whether it was because he had not managed to keep his small family together on the farm and could not give enough time to a growing child no longer living in the neighbourhood. A child who now stayed with a mum and stepdad instead of visiting him. Guilt, because he was no longer living up to the standards he grew up with, no time to fit all the jobs in or to serve the creatures he lived for, to the standards he considered their right – an agreement made with ancient mankind – the reason for farming in the first instance when mankind and animal came together for Mutual Benefit. The erosion of this agreement hurt him badly and he was no longer willing to march that route. To Peter the dead end of farming lay in that poor sentiment, somehow he would find a better way.

Expert knowledge of other forces was the strength of that most charming creature. The Voice, she, or maybe it was a he – no matter – had some sort of alter ability to keep the everyday forces away far enough and long enough for Peter to experience another world completely. That he had heard of this world in the stories led by Margaret, and he had known her and listened to her since childhood, still the similarities between what he was experiencing and what Margaret had elucidated over the years had not come together in his mind as one and the same thing. Probably it was due to the fact that with actual experience, and its description in words, even with the added embellishments of waving hands, cigarette and expressive vocalisation, somehow, a miss is as good as a mile, and missing the point can so easily be done by any of us. So Peter's internal journeyings were on his own scale and rankings. So similar in texture to Margaret's mutterings had he actually been forced to describe them to somebody, but Peter had no other body to outpour to. Perhaps that was a good thing, because Peter may have been ridiculed or told that he was making it all up or dreaming, had he been in the mood to talk to some non-sensitive person whose system was stilted enough to receive only signals from the here and now.

This magical essence of belief can be broached by anybody. It comes as a matter of course with birth, lives in childhood a while and then with puberty is commonly sidelined and sent to the back of the mind, like a naughty child to the back of the classroom, to turn its face to the wall. Luckily for some, music, art – as mentioned before – and drama can bring its light to the fore and imagination creeps slowly back to a place of recognition as a skill, not a misgiving, when training in this quarter is taken seriously. Peter's training came partly because of his sensitivity to Margaret's feelings, allowing her stories to wash over him even when the other children had long gone from her home. She could tell him about her premonitions and likes and dislikes. She harboured wild animals, even alongside her cats and came into her own for a potion or two for ailments too slight or too sticky for modern medicine. She was what every village and community had once had, the wise woman, the witch, if you like that word, but she was also respected by the professionals she encountered in the Social Services world as she, and she alone guaranteed a changed child after her bout of treatment, when others' charges turned and returned to the dark side once free from the fetters of their kind of foster care.

Gentle Peter listened and appreciated her company even if he did not understand what was rubbing off onto him at the time; her legacy for gentle travel to other realms had come with Peter's change of heart on the farm. His fulcrum point allowed him through, his tinnitus a thing of the past, he was in charge in his own headspace and he utilised it to its full extent. This was where his loneliness was quelled for just a while. Here he felt totally joined to a world of love; expansive and knowing. It caressed his sensibilities as he made positive changes and he felt that ideas came to him easily. His confidence in himself was firming up with every day and decisions to join in more at a community level had made him just a little less of the one man band with only his Margaret for conversation. Margaret was gone now in any case. His relationship with biosecurity tamed and doable, his energies had risen and mended his heartsorryness. Now he had time for his fellow mankind and showed it in better conversation and accepting the occasional invitation off the farm.

A changed man, Peter in charge of his outer life because of his belief in the goodness and power of his inner life. One day he will put two and two together and see just how Margaret dared to happily row her own boat in the community, her inner strength was such that nothing from outside could or would shake her beliefs. Mad muttering Margaret, a loss to the village and all the animals in the surrounding area but a gain of mammoth proportions to her 'better place'. That place she was sure she would be taken once her earth job was over. Blessed Margaret, you won't smell there, unless it is of the good scent of roses, for you have bloomed and blossomed in your life and taken so many others with you on that growth spurt too.

The tying up of movement to activity is a weird one. The physical movement may be originated by an outside force – look at the tumbling down through rocks of a mountain stream whose water, reaching an edge just has to flow, to bounce and tumble, creating spray and ripples on arrival at the bottom. The bottom actually being an opposing force to that which created the tumble in the first place. Stop! says this force, or blast your way through me if you can. The pool at the base of a standard waterfall is just that, an accumulation of blasts from dropping water. The greater the height and fewer the impediments on the way down, the fiercer the opposition to the 'stop!' mode. Why this? You may ask, because this is also the basis for our story. Where will Peter stop falling, tumbling through emotion and outside force and begin to put in place his 'stop!' moment. Is it when the fulcrum point of 'cannot take any more of this' is reached, and how will his 'stop!' be manifested? There are some awful 'stop!' moments in the farming world. How can Peter create his 'stop!'?

Mentally he is already on his way, he has put in place an ultimatum for himself, and is taking tiny, tiny steps towards a different line, a new approach. The outside disturbances of subsidy are closing down for him. His, the decision to creep out from that particular noose. The family problem, his unwillingness to hurt others' feelings or rock the family boat have been broached and settled without undue friction or effort. He is still with us, Peter the farmer man, gentle, unbeaten for all the tumbling through rocks of his and not his own making. Gradually he clears the way for his own decisions in his own life to be the major factor in his progression. Still unclear of his future he at least makes way for one to appear. The ground is clear, the uncomfortable rocks and outcroppings avoided or cleared. Where will the stream of his life take him now? He is becoming the active force in his own life.

Let's look inside, each one of Peter's atoms has been straining with this change – remember the man who hung his head, who sweated his way through the sale of his cattle and awoke scared and confused with what his mind was throwing at him. Now, clutter cleared, his step is lighter, weigh yourself man, have you lost those extra midlife pounds – no. His step is lighter because each atom, having given up the strain of painful living has lightened, has now the ability to rotate more freely on its axis, to create its own little buzz of excitement at being alive. No longer accumulations of brooding darkness gather in his spleen, spitting and balking at the unfavourable jobs and unreasonable demands of a too crowded life, overworked, tired, unmessaged, just repeating again and again the same routine but with no joy. That is when the darkness accumulates and attacks the organs of life.

Unhealthy living cannot be blamed here, our man is outdoors in the fresh air, a usual panacea for good health, his diet is basic and good, another healthful pointer and it is never lack of exercise that is bowing his limbs or hanging his head. No, it is pressure from without and pressure from within, conflicting pressures causing bursting atoms, bursting cells and night times with poor quality sleep, or little sleep where repair cannot take place, hence accumulation of little hurt after little hurt – the equivalent of the waterfall being forced to spray, fragment and tumble. To arrive out of place and never have time to recover before the next onslaught of disarray, worry and financial concerns come Peter's way. A cycle that somehow needs to be stemmed, sorted, smoothed out and Peter has started. The repair is now beginning to show on the outside. The lightness of step, the whistle that escapes his lips from time to time, just tiny symptoms of things to come, of Peter taking the direction of flow of his own life in hand. No, he does not as yet know or understand where he may be led, for he will be led. His intuition will lead him forward to a better place because he is now taking charge and once the ribbons of gloom are unwrapped and he can remember the Peter that used to be, he will be stretching his hand forward, happy for assistance from wherever it comes. Ideas will again be able to flow through a brain less cluttered with worries and sleep, soft recuperative sleep will disperse the bruised and damaged cells of his body, freeing up each tiny atom to whiz and sing and zing in happy response to this freedom. Peter's thoughts turn to the future. His ideas are somehow loosened from the tight moorings that previously constrained him, channelled him through someone else's idea of how his farming business should be run, in those days when he was told what was logical, sensible, financially self-appreciating. But this information was the very closing down of his joy. The logic was totally opposed to the sense he could feel in his chosen profession. Farming is never about wanton killing. Farming is not a soft profession, killing is a part but that killing is as a result of a harvest not an unwanted product that nature has to give in order to get the other. Which is it? Was that boy calf the unwanted by-product of this dairy farm? Or is the milk the by-product of a birth? A real live calf brought struggling to the surface of life to breathe and be cared for – these conflicts are the rocks and impasses of Peter's old life. Let him go, let him care for his animals how he can, without pistol in hand, unless it be used as a mercy tool in case of accident or emergency, never the private emergence of a life from the womb. That is sacrilege and Peter felt it hard. This was the incident that damaged his life. That he had gambled and been caught out, that was where his shame lay – sacrilege, and his grandmother would have also cried at this scene.

It lay behind him now, Peter was now mending, he changed his way, restructured the farm to suit his sensibilities and although the scar from that incident had not yet faded it had been a catalyst for change.

Chapter 11

The calm restored and work a pleasure,
Peter dares to have some leisure.

Peter sat at the table looking at the array of paperwork in front of him. It just struck him as ludicrous that in order to run a farm which was mainly outside work that there was just so much flipping paperwork to keep up with indoors. The thing is, when it is blowing a gale and raining and all your clothes are dripping, the hat rack is a row of bedraggled sogs and even your socks have not survived staying dry – come inside, get changed, a good warm cup of tea, look at the paperwork and immediately nod off. It is just not compatible!

Indoors is for relaxing, outdoors for working. Whoever thought men of action could make the change? All those office types, they stayed indoors and did their work, no one said to them 'now get outside and muck out a shed' – they would probably complain they weren't suited. So what made it OK that folk like him, practical guys, were supposed to be able to change their colours just like that and take on board a whole lot of la-di-da words all of a sudden. It was not that he was stupid, far from it, but he just was not suited. Added to which it felt somewhat meaningless, whose idea was it to have to stick all these great big tags in cattle ears anyway? If it was to identify a carcass at the abattoir, well, the head got chopped off anyway! So who is playing jigsaw with cattle heads and bodies after that? Don't tell me that mistakes aren't made.

Bigger farms might have a dedicated office worker who got the hang of the paperwork. He felt as if he had to relearn it each time he used the computer and the blooming keypad was too small for his giant fingers. Pressing down two keys at once was an occupational hazard with him – his occupation had given his hands their muckle size, the hazard was that he spelled everything wrong! It was all so long-winded with him. The words swam in front of his eyes and several times he jerked himself awake just before his head landed on the desk in front of him. He registered some calves. Painstakingly, with jabbing single fingers wrote a couple of emails and confused himself by losing everything at least once. There was no visible logic to this computer stuff, at least not the sort of logic where the problem can be sensibly worked out. You knew where you were with a lump of wood, some nails and a hammer, in fact taking a hammer to the computer would actually give quite a lot of satisfaction but he would probably regret it afterwards. Fortunately Peter was not a hot-headed man otherwise he may well have.

Sleep got the better of him, paperwork abandoned he succumbed to the armchair for forty winks, the modern day power nap! In this fine state, hanging between sleeping soundly and daytime awareness, lies another world for Peter. This is his playground now. He has chased away the gremlins that used to haunt him, achieved an equilibrium in his workplace that allows his sensitivities towards his animals' needs to be fulfilled well enough for peace of mind and now his relaxed mind dares to do other than grumble at the state of the world around him. Beauty is creeping back in. Gradually a new set of values are drawing themselves towards him, a tolerance towards his fellow man – even the stupid ones, maybe especially the stupid ones because they can't help it. His quality of life had changed so drastically lately he could really hardly believe it and with those changes had come some surprising revelations. He realised that the scale of the important things in life had got out of hand. Efficiencies had gone beyond their efficient boundaries and tumbled into chaos. Did he have any solutions to these problems? He thought not, at least not at the sharp end of any of the problems. He couldn't sort out the energy crisis or the health crisis, but he did feel empowered to deal with his own situation now. The endless muddle of running to catch up with himself had eased, perhaps he never would get the paperwork up to date or even up to scratch but that was because he was not suited, and it was a half-cocked system anyway. But other parts of his life had pulled together, he felt inventive again, ideas flowed in him. A cleanliness to the lines of his farming, a sense of pride for the new things he planned. Not for riches but for healthy animals, happy animals. That made the big difference in his life and those aspects had knock-on effects when it meant fewer vet visits. In the old way the vet visits had been either routine, because of government rules or panic stricken events when he couldn't sort a problem himself. Now under his new regime he hardly ever needed to make the panic calls anyway. He had made changes and survived, made changes and thrived. A sigh of contentment escaped from his lips, he snoozed on for a few more minutes happy to give himself that pleasure, and memories of Margaret rose in his mind.

Coming from a stable upbringing is one thing, but when Life has been chaotic all around you it is very difficult to sort out the important things from the fripperies. The boys that Smelly Margaret looked after usually came with a head full of nonsense. Funnily enough they had a good grasp on hierarchy, gang warfare had firmly placed that as an important line to be drawn in their minds and they all dreamed themselves at the top of that particular tree. Margaret used this familiar trait in the boys to help steer them into a good life. Once her boys had been with her for a few days, they could sense a routine was in place, always breakfast, lunch and tea, not dinner, tea as it was firmly called. The youngsters who had been there a while and had the house rules under their belts so to speak, also got privileges. This was a little like a ranking system in the army. It was earned, not fair to say that it was by good behaviour, because Margaret could see that some of her little chaps had a long way to come before being polite or sensitive to others' feelings was something they understood as a worthwhile mission to achieve. This ranking had no structure from the outside, it was measured on a one to one basis by Margaret herself and it consisted of tiny treats and privileges. One being that a 'trustworthy' boy would be sent to the village to buy Margaret's ever loved cigarettes. Now this may seem an odd treat but Margaret needed those 'gaspers' to keep her own equilibrium in a household that was disrupted by various issues on a regular basis and she also knew that she could put just an extra few pence to the money that this privileged youth took with him. A whispered, 'and something just for yourself' as he was going out of the door, out of earshot of other children was the signal that this boy had earned his colours.

It was an unwritten rule that this was kept secret from the others. A quiet system of rewards, not something that could be faked, no sucking up in order to gain rewards but a quiet nod in the right direction and this tiny private 'howdy – you are doing well' from the muttering Margaret was the biggest prize that any of these lads could ever receive. Being praised may never have entered their lives before and Margaret was no soft touch but when she sensed or saw a change, a softening of the exterior armour-plated hard boy image, she was there like a shot, but privately. Private praise meant that this young boy could savour that feeling of being trusted, of being rewarded and within a little glow, a glimmer of something started. Gradually the quiet revolution of senses happened, a responsibility towards the other children coming through the door, the bringing down of the barriers to communication, communication that before had been painful or irrelevant or misunderstood. Here the signals from Margaret were very clear. No matter who you are, or what you have done or do, even now here in Margaret's home you are worth a good solid home, meals and the opportunity to learn – when there was the slightest evidence that the learning was coming from the boy's side, then the rewards began. Up until then all the basics were there. There were no lectures about good behaviour, no holding another aloft as a good example, so that no one should feel the lesser, but just little ways that Margaret could quietly show her appreciation of a turnaround in sensitivity. She would squeeze a shoulder on the way past if she saw a young lad, previously unaware of another's feelings, act with compassion for a homesick boy, for there were tears and tantrums. Margaret was called all sorts of awful names, the countryside where she lived was deemed boring, nothing to do – that was until the magic started to rub off, and the cat had conquered the heart of the boy, or another had stood up for the cat against someone less loving to 'dumb' creatures.

Gradually outdoors began to hold fascination for

the lads, trees were climbed, and fallen out of, sometimes there were bruises. Footie even with fairly wrecked balls was a favourite and then, treat of treats. The lads who had been there the longest and had gained Margaret's trust were allowed a packed lunch, just a plain sandwich in a bag, and freedom to roam until tea time. By the time these young boys had risen in Margaret's estimation enough to be honoured with this treat they were changed children and actually instead of being thrilled at the prospect they were slightly apprehensive. After all, they arrived all streetwise and false confidence, and with Margaret's special care and treatment, they had had their childhoods returned to them. Most likely their schoolwork would have taken a turnaround for the better, no one was asking them to be top of the class, but a basic writing and reading skill was a big ask for these youngsters who came with a degree in cheekiness and backchat. Now they were being sent out to look after themselves for a whole day and to use their new-found sensibilities on their own terms. Margaret's haven may have been scruffy but it was home, and behaviour, as the new boys arriving demonstrated, was the standard they had grown up with. This was different, to be out and about and know how to be 'good' was a trial. They understood enough to know that this may be a fairly underpopulated part of the countryside compared to the heaving masses of city or town life where they came from but, here, whatever they did and wherever they went, they were recognised. No hiding in the melee of street life but exposed and solitary, with the chance that someone would be watching what they did and no doubt judging, ready to report back to Margaret. In all this the biggest watcher of all would be themselves. These lads were learning to judge their own behaviour, for when they were on their own they had new standards to adhere to. If they were in the ranks of lone travel then they were also trusted to have good enough judgement to understand the rules of the countryside. Margaret's hopes were that these boys would one day find those rules, adjusted for town or city life, would be the moral basis from which her lads would grow, meanwhile – watch out for bulls, keep away from cows with calves, if you have to open a gate, shut it behind you or climb over the gate at the hinge end and have fun without hurting or harming anything.

Margaret asked them to bring her back a treasure from their adventure too. These treasures she arrayed on the mantelpiece above the fire. It was cluttered with stones and feathers and sometimes a rusty gate hinge. Clever Margaret, cigarette in hand, in her muttering ways, would, as part of her routine when boys were being rowdy or squabbling, stand by the fireplace and select an object. She would mutter on about which child had brought her what and how it had come from such and such a place and how he'd walked three miles and where he had been and what birds or creatures he had seen along the way. Muttering Margaret would gradually attract an audience from within the squabble. She could identify which bird the feather had come from and tell stories about the habits of those birds. She would praise up the child whose gift was on the mantelpiece and Clever Margaret chose the gifts from children now returned into their new lives. She could only hope that her special treatment had rubbed in deep enough to make a difference in their life. She never spoke about a gift given by a lad still in her care. That was part of her therapy. The quiet reward system. Having the freedom to roam, and the honour of having an object displayed on the mantelpiece was enough, and those for whom this was still to come were never obliged to compete with a child who still stayed with Margaret by giving what might be considered to be a better gift. Clever Margaret avoided comparison among anyone still under her care. She knew she was not bringing up angels but also understood that each child must work towards his own personal good for this to be a meaningful exercise and the boys arriving had no conception in the beginning just how thrilled they would be when their particular artefact would have the height of respect on Margaret's mantelpiece.

Clever Margaret, she turned those boys around and cleverer still she praised their achievements from afar to an appreciative audience captured by her stories. She clothed the simple found feather of a long returned-to-his-origins foster child, with the golden glow of achievement whilst at the same time imbuing in any receptive mind the glory of the natural world where such a humble and easily found gift was gleaned. Clever, clever Margaret, who taught you? Peter smiled at his snooze-time memories and thought, 'Plenty of time to go and get wet again and plenty of opportunities too.'

Now, with his internal sun shining and his mind free from the clobbering effect of the past, Peter felt he could breathe again, and what breaths he was taking. Deep, long, like the strong strokes of swimming he did in his youth, when cares had not yet come upon him and 'the future' figured not in his psyche. To talk of his psyche, what a vista had opened up. He felt as if he had his feet, or at least his mental feet planted in two worlds. This one, the everyday place where he grew up, this place that threw challenge after challenge at him and in the past he floundered at how to cope, to face and overcome the challenges. Now, with access to this, his 'quiet side', as he had named it to himself, there was a refuge and that is where he took his challenges. He no longer stormed in, huffing and puffing and muttering under his breath about how typical that this or that should have befallen him when already he had enough on his plate. He had cleared his plate, not always with relish but with a sense of duty, a sense of enjoying the order that came into his life once the distasteful task was surmounted. In essence, the joy of the calmness of order outweighed the difficulty of the task. It was the seesaw effect again. Prepared to tune himself to 'order', he had to cross the special place, the magic of the fulcrum and he learnt to hover there, hold that space, the No Time, No Where place long enough to glean the strength, the courage to move onto whatever task was placed ahead of him. Then Life surprised him by offering solutions, sliding them in sideways. The time he had at long last decided to take that particular bull by the horns and make himself understand the position he was in with the farm. Uncertainty had blocked his creativity, worry about a negative outcome, or a falling out within the family that this gentle soul could not countenance, had held him back. Now with his new-found courage and bravery his common sense told him that looking into his affairs was not only sensible but he also had the option to do nothing anyway. Nothing need change unless he wished it to. Nobody was pushing him on this.

In his half waking half snoozing state Peter found himself at peace, catching onto the tail of an idea, one that seemed to be building and not yet coalesced enough to be properly formulated or visible enough to act upon.

The original goo growth carried about on boot and trailer, dispersed itself far and wide, the disinfectant routines on most farms quelled it and it soon died away, but the government controlling measures were deemed to stay in place for a while, during which minimal movements were carried on farm to farm, and visits were closely considered for their purpose. Coming off the farm was not such a problem, wheels were cleansed and wellies dunked before travelling but all this segregation did add to the general feeling of loneliness. Peter had solved the problem of petty thefts; he rigged up a post box and parcel drop-off point in a gateway partway down the drive, security felt better there and he put a decent disinfectant point here too. Familiarity with this event had taken the strain out and word from above of the non-virulent nature of the problem just meant it was more of an inconvenience than a burgeoning unknown problem-to-be. Unwanted though, it still meant that incoming feed could be spoilt if contamination got out of hand so vigilance was key and most farms and similar rural businesses were on their guard.

All the while, secretly the Little Mutation was recovering his strength, his new shape had helped, squirted him out from underneath the attacker's grip like a greasy pig. Near but without touching him, the attacking disinfection passed. Certainly there was something that had struck through the normality of this situation, his spin was always skewed now, away from the common goo which gave in so easily to heat or fierce burning chemical attack. He slipped and slithered through the trial, the burning substance now diluted, absorbed and dissipated over time, wended its way ever down the gravity gradient towards a drain, a ditch, there to further dilution. Our Little Mutation, left high and dry, still alive on his own terms, to rest a while, regain strength from some invisible source, the self-same source that had supplied the effort to change in the first place. A man among millions, or trillions or more, but wait, not a man, but a tiny Life, a living thing straining with the effort of staying alive, living quietly in a ditch. It caused no problems and bided beside the milliard other bacteria and microorganisms that make up the working world. We have all survived together in this bacterial melting pot since the dawn of time. What was different now? Nothing for most organisms but this, the newcomer, new kid on the block was keen to strain again at the edges of where he had come from and influence his evolution as much as possible. To this end and away from the ultra-drying effects of sunlight, there on the damp tidemark of Peter's hosings our little fellow squeezed the last ounce of effort from his frame and bursting with pride peeled open his personal sheath; swelled, proud and open to further chances and change. Clever, once done this was a replicable event. Choosing a compatible atom from his surroundings there in the damp, and there were many possibilities, the one that matched his spare little space, heaved itself into a position of comfort. A magnetic shift in the pair had made a mutual attraction not dissimilar to the attraction borne of hormonal desire like love can produce. Conditions shone just right for this pair and exactly that, a pairing was made. The duo became a compound and the tiny little lives within changed again.

In the way that oxygen and a couple of hydrogens make a threesome and become the completely unique substance of water, with its own rules, regulations and states of matter, so, our original Little Mutation, already changed enough to avoid the burning yet not-destroying approaching scorch of chemical disruption, strived again to make a mutual mating. This event chimed in with a substance so common in the world that we rarely register its being all around us, within us and of us. The most basic of the solid, liquid and gaseous world we live in, that hydrogen atom pushed back the limits of what had formerly been possible and jumped into a new role. A new possibility was born and the original substance of the goo changed forever, moved on, evolved. Its own primeval moves being made in a matter of months not years or millennia, so it goes on around us all the time; hit and miss, noise and the drowning out with white noise, waves building and breaking in constant motion. This time two meet and build, build, build, a little virtuous cycle, positive feedback loop as one builds on the success of the other. A new tiny, yet potent microorganism is born, happy to sit and wait for the next adventure to begin.

And what a happy adventure this is to be.

Chapter 12

*With spring in step and forward look Peter is learning
how to cook up future dreams and make a start on
Life lived truly from the heart.*

Down here in the depths of Peter's mind a wonderful change was taking place. Mind? Brain? Which was it on the change? The brain, physical grey sloppy cauliflower of cleverness, hidden within a cranium, so important to the Life running the show that it needs full armour plating. Even the pumping heart only gets a bony cage for protection, so brain is obviously right up there in importance, but where is Peter keeping his mind? He can change his mind, at the drop of a hat but cannot change his brain, or can he? Yes, his brain does change in the natural recycling of living cells that regenerate this living frame inhabited by Peter, but within, Peter can exist in his mind without conscious feeling interaction with his body. He strains his brain to think, but are the thoughts already there, queued up, waiting for the physical brain to reorganise itself? Waiting for this brain to form a conduit to travel through, like the directing walkways for queues at the post office made with rolled out separators, movable, adjusted according to the number of the waiting customers. Perhaps like check-in at an airport where the line of people file past each other first in one direction and then another, passing like well-choreographed lumbering dancers, baggage in tow.

How do we square this conundrum? Peter's brain rearranging the posts and lines, creating walkways to direct the travellers and customers. Peter's mind already awash with new ideas just waiting for the merest slimmest space to rush through. Complete ideas already formed in a mind existing without the brain. Brain needing the training and freedom to expand its range enough to allow and accept the new. The lumbering baggage-laden travellers too zombiefied and stuck in their ways, only able to travel the well-worn everyday brain paths. Hypnotised by complacent familiarity, unable to fly unless they take someone else's idea and hang on it like the heavy appendages they are, weighing down the walkways with their stomping ways. Brains need not be like this. A child brain, full of imagination but not yet fully trained, accepts learning unprejudiced from all comers. Older children then use their brain's filter of training to accept and discard, add in new information and embellish with their own creativity, a healthy mix of training and mindful creativity. Rules, while a reasonable demand for roads and ball games, need not also thwart the natural flowering of mind which is there, just hanging everywhere, to be pulled into work whenever a new problem needs a solution. Open the way for the mind by training the brain, but do not close the brain down with overtraining – lest the danger is in believing the training. Oh! the world of Paradox appears again as if by magic. What is good turns upon itself when overused, or twisted from its original message. Training is man-made exercise to stretch and motivate. Train to gain.

The wonderful thing about ideas is, that, if it is possible to have one, another even better may come along to displace it. What a wonderful thought already. Mind is not brain, the child lives in touch with his mind, open to all, not ruling out the magical, the seemingly impossible because perhaps somewhere the impossible is possible. In this world, the lumbering may sit on the aeroplane and be flown, barely a century ago that was an impossible dream. Today the mobile phone can give face to face access to a friend across the ocean, no more than an impossible nonsense to our grandparents when they were young. Never rule out an idea. Unproven yet, it is only something to be strived for by rearranging the posts and ribbons in the brain, in order to give free rein to a mind burgeoning with possibility, pushing for the new, aching to be believed sensibly and straining to give proof, to find an opening and shoot through an incredible idea to astound the disbeliever. Take the scissors, cut the tapes, ignore the lumberers and skip between them on light feet. Show the newness of ways to come, move to the front of the queue and launch the idea gifted from the mind. It can carry strength and a new future into manifestation.

As the brain cells regenerate and the brain is renewed in a time zone of the body's making, so the mind when unfettered can fly at speeds well beyond that of the aeroplane full of lumberers. Only catch this modern new plane and set foot there if the willingness for change is genuine. There will be struggles on the way, turbulence, but also new horizons for those with long vision and children to care for. Join the force to come. Return the letter that asks you to sign your life into the rut, the boarding pass to boredom and mediocrity and pick up the passport of possibility. Create your own design with open minds skimming along on trained brains into a human scale future of common sense proportions and sustained resources. Give up the old me, me, me attitude and accept that to be a unique individual among many is where the greatest strength and creativity lies.

Now Peter has his own mind to play in, he allows time to be on his side and takes pleasure in the ideas that come to him. It is still his to work things out, he needs to refurbish buildings and his mind will insist on gifting him the idea of buildings beyond his purse. Between them, his common sense brain, calculator in hand, agreeing only once the sums are done, and his mind, flying kites of fantastical proportions, the work gets done. Here is where the art comes in, and, practised now, Peter can look at the grander picture without chastising himself for being unrealistic; instead he takes what he can from it to furnish his modest needs sensibly. He orders new materials and stays within budget, feeling pleased that the farm is on the move again towards a future in which he has some hope and personal responsibility. Quite where he is going with this is yet to come to the fore, there are bigger ideas below the surface, biding their time. Now they have Peter's attention with the flagged-up out of scale crazy ones, these new ideas are also confident of getting through to Peter via his brain as and when they are needed. Let them through Peter, your helping hands are reaching out to cooperate.

The force of the ideas comes from a place that Peter is just learning exists. He was a stuck person before, when he was given farming-by-numbers to do. He was told when to sow and when to reap and the gains from his harvest were meanly distributed. The largest share went to those who had little to do with the farm, who sat elsewhere, maybe even in a yacht in the Caribbean just pressing buttons that affected Peter, who was scurrying hither and thither trying his best to keep up with the demands that he had signed up for, knowing only that without his meagre share all would be lost. Never having time to draw breath and think his way through a problem. Problems came thick and fast and the advisors only had platitudes about 'the future' to shove in his direction. Phew! Exhausted every night, no longer even time to get himself adequately washed and cleaned up before the next round of demands on his time arrived. He hated the moments when the calves had to go, but at the same time was relieved just for a day or so that it was one less job to do. The only problem being that there was the cleaning up in the calf house to get on with and seeing this building close up reminded him of the lack of maintenance he was able to achieve on his income. Income that hardly even covered his costs and with the demands of his 'sponsors' to meet, a designated feed company, a designated set of calf rearers to service, it was all by numbers. He could not put his foot down and say, 'actually I have found a better source of feed, or a more trusted calf rearer whom I know personally and will do their best by my animals'. No, his world was dictated to from outside the farm, but with what seemed like an immovable hardness, incompatible with what he had expected from a farming life when he had been so keen to join up.

Peter, now with some time on his hands had calmed down, the inward turmoil of overwork and worry was settling into a quieter routine. He breathed into his work a love and solidity of manner as he took stock of what he owned and weighed up in his mind how he might achieve the dreams of his youth. Farming, what was that to the Boy Peter? The animals were number one; he loved the animals, all of them. He thought of the ones he was up close and personal with, the cattle, sheep – he had none now but it was a mixed farm when he grew up, room for sheep in the fields, and pigs, just one or two, mostly to service the family, fill the freezer and share with friends. The dog, he had no need for a dog now, just another mouth to feed. But he loved dogs, missed their loyal friendship and fun. The cats were still around, a definite necessity, the rodent control patrol, the night guards.

There were more animals to think about too, the wild animals. He thought back to the leveret and wondered, hoped, that he, or his relatives were thriving in the meadow. The shy animals: newts, lizards, myriad bird species, glimpses here and there but knowledge of how full nature is, was always with Peter. His fields brimming with little energies interlocking in symbiosis and working their way up the food chain from lowly worm and grasshopper, through the little field mouse and frogs to the hawks and owls he heard and saw, the day and night flyers. The scallywag rabbits and their stoat foes to rebalance the land, with fox and badger at the top of this particular tree. The trees hosting yet another set of symbiotic comfort for insect and bug life, supporting with shiny backed protein and buds and seeds. Oh, what a wonder and fullness this land of Peter's is when tended to, husbanded like Peter desires. He can now make time to look and study, to fill the gaps in hedges, make them strong and stock proof again. They become the natural highways and corridors for bands of squeaking long tailed tits and dormice to scurry in, keeping their heads low and hidden when hawks appear but also glad to give their share to make the world turn in this little heaven. Top of this tree is Peter, once this land fully feels his care it shall flourish and its richness shall furnish him with pleasure. Keep your yacht, there is pleasure in this re-floating of a farm again after the disaster of the Pirates of the Caribbean have had their grasping far-off hands filled with Peter's treasures. They raped, pillaged and violated without mercy. Peter gladly hands back the money, the gold they crave, happy instead with the diverse richness of his natural world. Just let him work in his world, gather in the harvest at hand, sell it close by, where his money makes sense to his community. Like when the pig was shared among the neighbours piece for piece, he understood his commerce, it made human scale sense to him. This is the farming he remembers and enjoyed.

But Peter is no longer stuck, neither is he stuck in the past. That farming of his boyhood drew him in, now he knows it is different and it can be as different as he is willing to make it. There is his challenge. Forming a new way, a new manner of farming to suit him, his gentle consciousness and his pocket. There is the pondering taking place and as yet no definite outcome from his mind has been presented, but

Peter is a patient man. Peter is not a hot-headed man and can wait, bide his time. He has his cushion and recognises it allows him just to rest, to repair his little farm and his personal hurts, his ravages from the past, his raped sensibilities. All this needs a little time to begin to heal, to soothe. Meanwhile, one thing is certain, Peter will get a dog. He may be lonely on the farm now but Dog will cheer him and give him an aim. Train to gain, his dog will be trained and another oneness formed. Gradually the scars fade and life moves forward in its flow, leaving the river of the past, the murky waters clearing now as Peter takes control of his life at last.

Make your mind up Peter, it is ultimately up to you to clear the decks of past created reality and bring another to the fore. But not everything is of your own making, you are only a small part of a whole desperately trying to turn the tide, but unlike Canute who unflinchingly stood to hold back an incoming tide by himself, to prove a personal point, you Peter can bring about these changes because of an idea you hold dear, an idea bigger than yourself, that of Farming. Farming as the idea formed generations ago. This Mutual Benefit, the kind of relationship that has a balance and fairness inherent in its structure. Mankind needs food, you, dear cattle are our converters, we cannot manage this land on our own, we need your guts to do the work for us. We used to follow you on your journeys to find grass, new grazing spots in the open plain but that was also troublesome for you. Your smallest beings, your children, the calves, struggled to keep up and the hyenas hung out near the watering holes and captured those weakened by the journey. You had to know where and when to travel and we made an agreement. You would sacrifice what we, your predators, would take anyway – food for ourselves. Our part of the bargain was to guard you from the wild animals, tend to you when you were sick, save you from scorching heat in our man-made shelters and store up fodder for winter, alleviating the need for both of us to trek so far for food. This we did together, you agreed, and for a while mankind was grateful. As grateful as ever to be allowed food, we gave thanks and did our best to care for you but then gradually this seemed easy, complacency reigned and the advantages on mankind's side began to outweigh the Mutual Trust.

Mankind, we, have forgotten that we need you to harvest the land for us and to produce the manure to make the future crops grow. We forgot that this agreement was made when mankind was much

much closer to the land, when an unwritten agreement meant something because the heart is like a book written with indelible ink and since then mankind has come up with the idea of writing on paper and screen. Once the writing is no longer inscribed upon a heart, there is a possibility to falsify the records, to cheat and lie and make claims of greatness where none lie. This earth is home to many creatures, some dying out and some, like our Little Mutation, coming into being. It is not for feeble mankind whose cleverness has allowed lies and distortions to be invented, no, not for mankind to judge who and what deserves good treatment on earth. Earth can find her own balance and happily engenders new growth to live on the vestiges of the old; the earth holds that record in her fossils. But mankind has tilted and twisted to his own ends and is running before he can walk and now it is time to make amends. The earth will always rebalance. The thing is this, do we wish our children to be there in the balance? If so, we must start now, look for the solutions and there is a place to find them. Scars will always exist but also may hold the key, the reminders, to keep the human race on track. Which will you strive for? Canute like, your own personal position, unflinchingly going under with the incoming tide, or will you compromise, build a raft of natural materials and float gently in with a tide of sustainable living, bringing your children with you, teaching them to be less needy for themselves and more caring within the group they find themselves? Remember, to be a unique part of a crowd is a forward flowing aim. The possibility is there, the technology in place for us to learn and share, to remember our hearts and the place where we made that agreement, that Pact for Mutual Benefit and extend it outwards through farming to our planet. She happily supports us... or dumps us. The choice is ours to make.

A new chapter in Peter's life has started, he can now concentrate again on the future instead of running fast to catch up with himself and this is just such a pleasure. He has bought a dog and it sits patiently by his feet, it amuses him with mad moments of energy and brings a smile to Peter's face more often than he was used to. This is all good news because internally changes are also taking place. Peter does not realise what a train of events have started all because he has taken his own destiny in his hands. He did not look for the easy option and he had to take risks along the way. Giving up his 'lifeline' of subsidy was not a decision he thought he would ever make, but subtle changes in the way it was presented, sinister snatching back of privileges he had presumed to be his right, that of making decisions within his own farm and small sneaking tweaks, meant his self-esteem and human sense of purpose had been eroded to such a point that he no longer knew whether being alive at all was an option he should be considering. If it had not been that he alone was there to feed and water the animals in his care he might have done that last and fatal deed and never have reaped the benefits that this life brings.

We serve life in a body of flesh, weighed down in physical matter, slowed up enough to have to make an effort to even move. This encapsulating is a form of limitation. Conjoined, the pains of the body are enmeshed with those of the mind and by smoothing out the path of one or the other, freedom to travel life's path is given. Time, that capricious ribbon, that road along which destiny forces one, plays its own tricks. Appearing to be a measure of before and after, it contorts to send intention ahead of the time performed by a ticking clock. Good intentions move the building blocks of ideas into place so that the traveller can take advantage of them. Put your intentions out ahead and watch the falling into place with seamless effort, or conversely charge the future with how difficult life can be and also this will be obliged. But it is not quite that simple, the hardest part of life is to hold onto the idea of good intention while what feels like disaster is tumbling all around. To falter at that moment is to flip the coin and make the tail fall where the head was aiming. Confused? Look again at your life and see that sometimes the hardest moments are the ones where most is learnt, most accomplished.

What is put into mind is never lost; mind stamped with personal achievement stays forever. A body is for life but a mind is part of eternity and carries evolution onward. Timeless, the Land of Idea knows it all, the matter of earth life in its slowness and inertia takes effort, but once the effort is made, that creativity is stamped unreservedly forever as an achievement to be praised or sometimes envied. It may be unrepeatable again on earth, but never need it be gone from the mind.

Chapter 13

*Excitement, new ideas abound, his life is
now a changing ground!*

Here the sun shone inwardly even when outside
the clouds covered the sky. Peter hailed to the sky like
a friend, acknowledging its need to release the water
held up there with the warmth and wind and motion
of exchange. The reciprocal action of life-giving
substance risen from the seas and given to the
mountain tops. It was along those lines that his
thoughts flowed. Mentally he made pictures whilst
carrying out his everyday tasks. He floated himself on
one of the clouds, dropped spinning to the earth and
joined a small brook tumbling downwards, hurtling
towards the sea. He allowed himself to free up enough
to enjoy the reverie, to become the child again, at least
within his mind. It refreshed him and made him
chuckle to himself as he worked, an involuntary
gentle whistling emitting from his lips. He heard it
like it came from elsewhere, once his awareness was
upon it he realised the tune came from him. A tune
from childhood days. Is it really that long ago that he
whistled? There was a lot of catching up to do.

He had all the materials assembled to rebuild the old calf shed, it was just a matter of finalising in his head which way to go. Peter never wrote things down, he was a man of action and ideas on the go, allowing inspiration to change his mind. He had learnt from previous mistakes that sticking too rigidly to a plan, especially some money focussed person's plan, copying what another guy did could be his downfall. This time he would do things differently, in fact drastically differently. He was nearly out of the regular milk market now, those sleuths had dragged him down. He still had a little money in the bank to lean on, and a bullock in the freezer, so he would not starve. You know, he thought to himself, I am going to bite the bullet and do the thing I have always wanted to do with my milk cows. For years he had had the heartbreak of removing the calves from their mothers at birth, or at least, after just a little suck of colostrum, that life affirming substance that could keep a little calf alive and on its feet no matter what else went wrong in its precious little life. He would do something dramatically different. He was not sure whether he had heard of a different method of calf rearing in other countries, or whether it was a dream-like type of wishful thinking, but he would just stop now, before the habit of rushing on and the familiarity of old ways pushed him back towards previous design. He would stop now, go and have a cup of tea and a good cogitate.

Hands round a steaming mug of tea, his ideas seemed to float from somewhere deep in his soul like the opposite of watching an object swinging its way to the bottom of a clear pool. Instead he 'watched' as ideas one after the other removed themselves from a jumble of dead leaves and other detritus and as if imbued with Life drifted upwards toward him. Ideas came as pictures, a calf snuggled up next to his mum, feelings of contentment and love as two creatures moulded by evolution and man's breeding, bathed in each other's gentle company. He knew his will could make this a reality. Then a picture of him in his parlour milking this same cow, Number 476. He 'watched' a stream of white milk gurgling through pipes... but how can that be? 'Surely leaving the calf with his mum means no milk for me?' His conventional training kicked in sharply – and it took a few moments for him to relax again, inhale the steam from his tea and allow his mind to settle back to the deepened reaches where his desire for change led him. He scrutinised the 'idea picture' again. This time he could see that cow and calf were actually separated. A stretchy canvas material came between them, forming a separating but flexible barrier. The calf leant into his mother's warmth and her rasping tongue reached over his back, languid but strong rhythmic licking motions rocked the calf's body, back and release, back and release. He sensed the strength of that natural bond, a recipe for good health and happiness. Suddenly it became a tangible possibility. Inwardly he smiled. 'Yes,' he thought, 'I shall do this my way. He can have his mum close by.' The first few nights they would be together, then this flexible barrier would be his ticket to some income from milk. He would introduce it in the late evening to begin with. Then as the calf was more able to cope he would increase the time of separation, but leave them able to communicate in the way cattle love, proximity and licks all over. Morning milk would be his. Number 476 could pay her way, and daytime milk and the full company of her calf would be the reward. 'Genius!' He carefully thought through the night time routine; mum and calf together, he feels the security and love of a mother, she gets to express her instincts, neither have to go through the trauma and grief of separation, and by default neither would he. An involuntary surge of relief and release cascaded through his body, his whole physicality changed in that instance. Without knowing or understanding it, he had held all those tiny portions of grief, for every calf he had forcibly removed from its mother, the pain in part was his – he breathed a silent prayer of thankfulness and in the same instant a wordless but potent apology to all the cows and calves put through 'that system'. Another thought crossed his mind, no more making up of that milk replacer. He never did quite 'get' that idea anyway. Buying in one kind of milk, industrial dried powder, and selling another, raw liquid. In fact, it might even have been milk from his farm that went to make the calf feed.

He was not actually sure where the milk from his farm went. It was out of his hands. He was simply a tiny cog in a huge machine. A number, a nothing when it came to it. The thought now pained him. He could no longer countenance that treatment of his calves. They could drink straight from their mums. Exactly the correct temperature, no in between times where contamination could get from the environment into the milk and no carrying slopping buckets in all weathers and no possibility of getting the mixture proportions wrong and causing scours. Yes, let's get to it, life is changing and for the better. In a flash he skimmed over all the positive aspects he had gleaned from farmer friends who kept suckler beef herds. Their cows, calves and sometimes even the bull lived together, regularly for sixteen years of healthy life. That's what he would aim for but with his milking cows. He would make this happen and why not?

The design could be simple, Peter was a practical guy, it would be no time before he came up with a way to make this innovation work and there was another satisfaction, inventing his new system with all the natural behaviours and instincts of his dear cows built in. He would do his very best to make a system for them that kept them in tip top condition, was not too arduous for him to deal with and brought in enough income to oil the cogs of the small farm he had made his home. A challenge he could be proud of. Bring it on, he thought, and mentally gave his best girl, Number 476, a friendly slap on the rump. In that instance another thought, exciting in its total simplicity. Number 476, that is no name for my favourite girl of the moment, from now on all my cows and calves will have the dignity of a real name. Peter chuckled to himself, am I getting soft? Am I reversing the trend in farming? Or is this just an honest human response to the connection between man and beast that has been fostered down the ages?

When were cattle first domesticated? He didn't know, but he felt it. I love my cows and I know they recognise me and understand what I need from them. I am pledging now to give them respect. No, I am not going soft, the understanding is that I do my very best by them and their offspring and they do their part. Milk and beef, that is their job. Kindly husbandry, that's my job and I know I have to abide by the laws of the land, ear tagging and records. I can do that happily.

Today is another cracker for our man Peter; he has blazed his way through his routine work, got new ideas in his head and is happy, happy, happy. He wishes only that he had someone who could share his triumphs. His good friend Margaret was the only person he was close enough to to be able to express himself fully, and she was no longer there for him. The change in her had crept up pretty slowly, almost imperceptibly, but Peter on his last couple of visits could sense her weariness. She mentioned that really she felt that she had completed everything that she needed to do here and was ready to be off. Peter didn't properly get the drift of her conversation and only when he heard through the grapevine that Margaret had died did the penny drop. Without Margaret, his happiness was tinged with a sadness too.

Margaret was cheerful to be gone. Her ailing body – possibly the cigarettes had eventually caught up with her – caused her problems and she was absolutely not going to get into the hospital's clutches, not Margaret. She would usher herself out with her own brand of dignity no matter what it looked like from the outside. She never had given much credit to other people's opinions, so nothing changed there. The crumbling house continued to give her enough shelter and neighbours, especially Peter, had kept logs and put warming dishes of food in front of her regularly. Her cigarette cupboard was still filled to the brim when she passed away, something she was very firm about. She would smoke to the end, and she did. A quiet passing in her own bed achieved, Peter was left to clear her things and seek out where her effects might go. It surprised Peter to find that Margaret had been as organised as she was. A folder with her wishes, deeds to her house, her bank accounts and a will were all easily accessible and Peter became the owner of a little tumbledown house not far from his own farm. Lucky Peter, your fortunes are shifting daily. All this, while easing for Margaret who had now gone onto her 'better place' still left Peter short of company, his animals fulfilled this part of him partially – a farm without animals is like a house without a family but he did crave human company. Soon this would change for him but that is for another day.

Peter's senses reeled with all the new beginnings in his life. He was enjoying himself, his new cow/calf experiment was keeping him busy but not overworked, and the slack with the expenses was a relief to say the least. Quite where he would go long term was still a bit of a mystery but that had never been Peter's sort of concern anyway. If it had been, then he would have made sure that he understood where he stood when Grandmother was obviously coming towards the end of her days. Fortunately for him, her diminishing years had brought her senses to a pitch where she had thought through a plan to keep Peter farming for as long as he was able. She had not told him, possibly she assumed he would know this, although telepathy had not been Peter's strong point then.

Now, however, Peter was noticing something strange in the way that he worked with his animals. He had always had a good eye for an animal and would certainly be able to tell whether any of his beasts were going downhill and do his best to counter the problem, but this was different. He had had an experience with a dry water trough, as if the unrest from those cows had alerted him through the ether or telepathically, and he had the experience with Margaret of eventually sorting out that troublesome drinking trough for good once he had seen the dowsing in action and done his repairs. He always felt good around his animals when things went smoothly but recently the level of peace and calm on the farm had surpassed anything he had known before. Why? He thought it through as he went about his tasks, enjoying being able to finish up little jobs that had irked him in the past, no unsightly piles of broken buckets and feed sacks lying around now, and in any case this biosecurity thing had brought all the farmers up short over that behaviour. Everyone, or nearly everyone, was keen to get clean and back to normal manoeuvres as quickly as possible and finish with the disinfectant routines.

It was this other feeling that Peter noticed from time to time. He broke through into a different sort of place, mostly when he was resting, a peaceful place. It felt as real as the here and now and it held knowledge because he always came away from there feeling good about himself and being able to solve any niggling problems. Sometimes it felt as if he had courage conferred to him. This new Peter socialised, met people, took time for himself, had even bought new clothes to feel confident and acceptable in a crowd. Yes, still farming ventures, of course, that is where he felt most at home but now he was contributing to society. He swapped ideas about machinery breakdowns and was offered the loan of equipment he did not own himself. It would take another big stride to take up these offers but knowing they were there comforted him. He felt part of a crowd and yet his new day/night cow/calf system was unique. He was still shy of talking about it, but that would come. Peter was rested up, and sensitivity followed him everywhere.

Today was special, he was meeting with a lady, a cheesemaker, youngish, single and single minded. There had been an advert in one of the local farming press magazines. 'Looking for a supply of raw milk – embryonic cheesemaking business' with a name and a telephone number. Peter was only too pleased to give a ring. Fewer cows meant a lot less milk and he was nearing the end of a milk contract. His was the least profitable farm on the route for the tanker driver and there were rumours about rescheduling pickups. Peter had given up worrying about such things. His attitude had changed to one of 'something else will fall into place – otherwise, plan B sell up and get out'. Those were his options and he lived at peace with them. He was not slack about the 'something else' part. He was willing to put effort into a new type of venture. He still had his cushion and his reduced milk cheque and was happy to be out of the iron fist of a subsidy. He was willing to give anything the time of day, to 'fly some kites' and mentally he felt freed up, light as air and open to new ideas. His heart was in his work, he had some time to be himself, order had returned to his life. A good sensible kind of order, not obsessive but tidy, uncluttered, safe. A good feeling.

Peter spruced himself up just a tad. A clean boiler suit and a shave, enough effort for one day. His boots were always clean, washed off after farm work and a separate pair for parlour work. This man took his work seriously, understanding the need for hygiene when working with milk. Milk was everyone's friend, every bacterium in the world loved to live on it or in it hence the attention to detail in the parlour. He was proud of his record there and it had improved since his major changes. Regular readouts on bacteria counts, buttermilk content and the rest, were part of his life and meant something to him. His new-found lifestyle had changed things for the better. She arrived, keen as mustard about the new business she wished to embark upon. A slight, dainty lady in her thirties. He enquired politely about where she had got the idea of being a cheesemaker from and she told him about her previous life in a busy, big town. A bursary from one of her jobs had allowed her to do a taster course in cheesemaking and she was hooked. Like him, she felt her life had 'careered' out of control. They laughed together at the pun. This really was a very new venture, one she felt she had all the energy and verve to follow through. Raw milk was where she would like to start, partly because she wanted to begin without investing hugely in pasteurising machinery until she was settled into a food making unit. Business start-up funds in place she was now looking for a source of milk but was completely vague about amounts, or regularity or anything really. What she had in bucket loads was enthusiasm and Peter got caught up in it. Potentially he had a little private contract with this budding cheese maker. Her interest was in the way that every cheese's consistency, taste and keeping quality came about with different ways of storing the milk; she even took the breeds of the cows into consideration. He just loved this holistic rounded attitude. At last things were falling into place.

Bang! Peter jumps! What is going on to disturb the peace of the farm? All the animals within earshot of this gunshot of a crack lift their heads from the grass, but just momentarily, for once the soundwaves die away, they are back to their work converting grass into Peter's income and your food and mine. But Peter is not so easily satisfied. His is not an inbred thought lying deep in his psyche of predator or foe, but more a curiosity for where that noise can have come from. Peter followed as best as he could, his memory of where he felt the eruption had emanated. He walked around the corner of a shed and there to his astonishment was a manhole cover pushed up out of the ground. Peter reacted to this unexpected sight with an uncontrollable bout of laughter. The crash had been the unleashing of this manhole cover, unshifted for twenty, maybe thirty years and grown in on all sides with grass and weeds. Junk had accumulated in this corner. It was Peter's stash of recyclable metals, currently a tangled heap, blown apart and in among it some sort of froth.

The aftermath of this explosion, and the shock of the disarray in this usually quiet corner of the farm took Peter by surprise, jolting out of him a laugh, a belly laugh, the first he had experienced for a while. As unexpected as it was ridiculous, Peter, once started, could not stop. He, there alone, beside this avalanche of chaos bellowed with a force enough to blow the cobwebs of his former despondency to kingdom come. Peter's life had changed, he was not in the predicament of the times before and inwardly he felt settled but still his habit of quiet solitude left him feeling down. This explosion was the loudest, most unexpected thing to have happened to him since some daft prank in boyhood and it gave him a boost. Hooray, Peter was still alive in there, not just marching through his duties one by one to get to the end of the day but truly alive. He had been bombed out of his complacency and into the immediate moment. Still he chuckled, and like a secondary reaction he then laughed at himself for succumbing to the first bout of laughter. In later years this was to be the event, where, if he were to even begin to relate it, he would already be in tears of laughter before he had explained why. The sort of thing where people would look at Peter and say 'I think you had to be there' and raise their eyebrows knowingly. But that is for the future. The explosion site found, Peter still had not ascertained the why of the explosion.

A back pressure from this froth had pushed and pushed at the line of least resistance. This manhole cover, less taut and dense than the surrounding concrete, with its seal of grime, grass and weeds had gradually given way to the force and blown the top off, showering up through the neat little sharings of copper pipe, aluminium sheets and old engine parts waiting for the day when Peter had time to take them for recycling, to weigh them in or reuse on the farm any odds and ends. The explosion had clattered the manhole lid through the pile, adding to the ongoing clanking as the pile readjusted itself to a new position. The froth, freed from its constraints settled back down, blown out, released and opened up to new conditions. This froth was the new incarnation of that goo. The new, turned, reshaped and able to avoid chemical disruption on that day a while before where the Little Mutation had lain, resting and then strained again and conjoined with something already good at shape shifting, at hiding in plain sight. The hydrogen was having a new incarnation too and bringing his explosive energies into being in conjunction with his new-found friend. Another change, another set of perfect surroundings and another site of tiny evolutionary success. Time and moisture and the achievement, escaping the original foe of burning disinfectant, to create this new and potent substance. The froth, now exposed, having done its job of releasing pressure died back, light and air popping its bubbles and shrinking it back to the drain where it had first emerged. Freed, but also fried and dried out of existence there in the open air. Its refuge the moisture of the drain, the remnants still living.

Peter was unmoved by the sight of the foam, his attention was taken by the bombsite of his recycling and the unexpected explosion of laughter. As the froth had found the line of least resistance, bursting out from under the pile of scrap metal, so Peter had burst spontaneously out of his deeply ingrained seriousness. The something in him, just waiting to burst, had pushed its way to the surface of his character well enough to be triggered by this shock, the unusual sight, this disarray. For Peter, better that the explosion happened harmlessly outward, an expression of his pent up and suppressed energies from the years of worry and care he had been subjected to. His release could have been a more permanent disaster, or it could have turned inward on him, distorting his inner self physically with disease or mentally with imagined distortions of his life. Lucky Peter, this froth has released both itself and yourself and may yet do you more good.

Chapter 14

This time at market, walking tall, his gleaming stock there for all to see and Peter proud to know his home-made system made them glow.

Peter was coming to the point where he must take some of his livestock to market, at least he chose that route rather than private sale, to claim a larger audience. His trailer, roadworthy and up to scratch, was duly cleaned and disinfected, a requirement for all farm vehicles these days. He was sure of his way to market avoiding the backroads where less conscientious rogue farmers flouted the rules on disinfecting, convinced that if they all pulled together over this last outbreak they could prove a satisfactory conclusion to the annoyance and extra work involved. Those brainless few, only thinking of themselves, were spoiling the lives of many. Often the way he thought to himself.

His stock was looking spectacular. He was proud of them, gleaming coats and an air of knowing. Strange to think that his belief system and confidence in his animals had grown, multiplied a thousand fold lately. It gave him such a sense of comfort to understand their way of thinking – of course he was never going to prove this to a modern day scientist with their reliance on fancy equipment. His confidence came from being in charge of his own complicated equipment. Right there in his bony old skull was his key to this knowledge and nobody, but nobody could take away from him what he had experienced. Nobody could share it either – a strange concept that. Living together, as we all do on this self-same planet, we all have totally differing experiences, plenty of crossover of events but that is not *experience*. He pondered a while, a few minutes to kill before the next little adventure, remembering some of his previous trips to market. He recalled cringing inside at the multiple grievances. Then, he had been stepping out into the unknown, reducing his stock because he had to. Knowing his offering would not be the best on the market but having to take what he could for them, unravelling that old life but uncertain where he was heading. Stepping away from the lifeline of subsidy that had underscored all his planning and advice from outside the farm. That determination he had felt, raw, knife edge, do-or-die stuff and here he was a million miles away from those feelings of doom, fear, aloneness. He walked tall. It was not a mish-mash of 'extras' that he took to market this time but young stock. He had his wonderful cows at home and they had produced for him this bountiful harvest. Thanks girls, an involuntary flutter of gratitude flooded from his heart, thanks girls. He felt a million dollars, his was a life so changed for the better he could hardly believe it himself.

Outwardly, the changes were obvious in part. His yard was neat and tidy, the vehicles clean, but they had to be with the disinfectant rules in place. His barn system completely revamped, cattle now choosing, to a degree, how they would be catered for. His day/night calving regime had worked well, but with fewer cows he could take time to explain the system to each individual, make a sort of mental agreement about what would be 'his' for farm and family, and what could be 'hers' for cow, calf and their combined wellbeing. He loved it, each cow had taken to this system easily, as if one had communicated to the other of the agreement – his respect for these animals' intelligence increased daily. The way to mark this intelligence was not the same as human intelligence. He could understand the feeling world of his girls much better these days. The air was thick with it, but he knew it was not air, but another type of substance, as real to him as air and as vital as the air he breathed if you talked in terms of wellbeing, of health and happiness rolled into one unspoken, but acutely held feeling. Oh how words were so inadequate to express this new-found aspect of living. It really felt as if his whole life, all the bad bits as well as the innocent bits were a training ground in contrast, for this kind of living. He still had surprises, he was not some kind of 'bliss-machine' but overall these were challenges with solutions to be found, inventions to be made and with the discoveries about his own and his cattle's inner workings, he could get round most problems within a day or two.

His inventions, how they had tickled him, presented themselves as solutions to small but urgent trip-you-up events. Like the time he had put one of his first day/night calving regimes into place. This particular cow had managed to sneak the calf under the separating material as if it were just an inconvenience rather than a carefully thought out plan for him to allow their closeness to be a comfort. When he arrived in the morning, cow and calf were cuddled up together chewing the cud – empty udder. The sight made him chuckle, clever girl he thought. Back to the drawing board. So his cow/calf separator, which he was determined was to be a flexible material allowing the comfort and feel of mum for security as well as warmth, had to be modified. This time he extended the bottom of the material and tucked it along the floor, placing a thick bedding of straw over it. This new design meant that the weight of the calf itself would hold the separator in place. It would get mucky, sure enough, but he would see to it that floor drainage shed much of the calf wee. He had looked forward eagerly to see whether this clever cow would be able to sneak her baby through. There was time enough to tweak the design, look out for tough waterproof material that he could keep clean. A triumph here, cow and calf together but separate and her udder obviously full, she would be glad of the relief of milking this morning.

The next part of the plan was how to manage the walk from night stalls to milking parlour without losing the milk along the way! Losing it in terms of the eager calf diving in before he had a chance to get to it himself, or losing it in terms of mum's reluctance to let it down properly. There had been no big hiccups there, a few judiciously placed hurdles guided the calf ahead of mum and once the clusters were in place, his dear cow stood calmly licking her baby while he collected his 'payment'. This was designed to be a mutually benefitting system for man and beast. After morning milking the pair were totally reunited, no restrictions, the calf dived in for a morning drink, and mum, stopping only briefly for this to happen was now keen to make her way out to graze, calf trotting by her side. Soon the milk would be flowing again and the calf had the whole day for topping up. There was no longer an evening milking, life felt leisurely now. The cows came in at dusk, settled themselves into a stall where they were offered an evening feed. While this was their main focus of attention Peter would slip down the lines and, scooping away the bedding with one foot, replace his patent separator and sweep the bedding over his ground flap. He soon got his routine perfected, shovelling the calf ahead of himself with his knees onto the 'dry' side without mother even noticing, her attention being on the trough in front of her. He loved these tasks, the closeness of the work, his expert eye taking in every nuance of movement, behaviour. This man would have noticed immediately should there be any problems physical or psychological in this perfect mother and calf pairing. No more crying, no more nightly bellowing, just a pair of contented bovines still in touch with each other. Love flowing as generously as the milk that was both man and calf's succour.

He ran to the end of this thought pattern and could feel the warmth of pride in his stomach. He wondered to himself whether he would be able to spot any farmer at market with the kind of problem he had been hiding. After all, then it had been him, chin in chest, eyes on the floor, but still with his expertise seeing others' stock for what is was. That is how his animals had reached a decent price last time, their underlying value shining through the immediate imperfections; too skinny, feet could be better, but a few months of TLC would soon sort that. Only he felt the shame of his animals' poor condition. It was the thought that some of those guys, it was mostly guys, at market would be holding the fear, the fright, the shame and was there anything he could or even would wish to do to help, to alleviate their inner turmoil? Maybe there was not, he had not been able to turn to anyone himself. There was recognition that problems arose in farming. The fact of loneliness, farmers worked on their own a lot. No longer a row of farm cottages full of workers, the inevitable hordes of children to annoy and enjoy in equal measures. He still had memories of farms like that. Now it was the postman, if restrictions allowed, and contractors, but who might they be? Possibly a different driver every visit, just time for a hello. Job to do, explain which field, any idiosyncrasies, a wet spot to avoid, the unusual placing of a poorly buried water pipe. Maybe a drive down in their cab to see the lay of the land together. Then, 'better way get on' and before you know it, a wave goodbye. Perhaps a short 'how do you do?' whilst washing the muck off the wheels. The rules for taking farm vehicles onto the public highways were tough now, but everyone has jobs to do off farm, and Peter had a very important off farm assignment to fit in after the market run.

It was a short walk for Peter, to be taking his former companion to one of the places she held in high esteem. Her ashes were in a humble cardboard box, she would have wanted it no other way, and once he stopped the vehicle and picked up the heavy little box he felt a shift within himself. Suddenly there was a dignity becoming to a serious ceremony of remembrance and although it was just him, alone on that hillside in the countryside that Margaret had loved so much, it felt as if the world had opened yet another door. He moved almost dreamlike in his reverence for the occasion he had been entrusted with. Possibly Margaret knew in advance what an effect this would have on Peter, because her knowing had gone beyond that of an everyday mortal. Margaret had lived from her inner core outwards while most mere mortals live from their outer shell inwards.

The normal state of being is to concern yourself with the trappings and rankings of life, the qualifications gleaned from mankind's store, the artefacts gathered in a lifetime. These are the things that so many of us set store by and look upon as treasures. Margaret, on the other hand, came into this world as tiny and bare as any one of us, but went out, this outing that Peter was witnessing now, she went out with a solidity of stature beyond anything that material possessions or rank or regency can bestow and Peter felt it right then. In those moments of walking, carrying what were a pile of dense ashes, the last physical part of his friend, confidante and ultimately his guru, had he but realised it. He walked with a new kind of stature, a solemnity befitting this last rite and passage of a woman who had broken so many rules of 'decent' living with her incessant smoking, her bashed up home and her individual way of working with the children who had come to her care. This woman, one of the last of a kind recognised only a few generations previously as a worthy part of community living, with her extra perceptionary ways, her people skills as potent as any modern psychologist and her remembrances of country lores and potions for ailments real and imagined, never hurting to human or land. She lived a close life, close to the land and close to her inner world. That inner world that she happily and continually shared with anyone within range of her muttering ways.

Dear Margaret, Muttering Margaret spilling her truths to anyone willing to hear, rubbing her goodness off on those who stuck around long enough to feel the power of her thoughts. She was not one to preach at you, her preaching and praise was for the wonderful natural world that she felt a complete part of. She could cry with you if you felt sad, and cackle a laugh at a friendly joke but most of all she spouted wisdom. To the skies, to the trees, to the birds and beasts of which her knowledge was legendary and here was Peter entrusted with that very reverent of occasions, ready to spill her last crumbs onto the ground that had fed her and been her playground and her companion and helper in her work, the difficult task of turning around children from challenging backgrounds where they had had no say in their inadequate upbringing. It was this very land that she had used as co-worker in her game of life;

friend, food, challenge and growth. She saw the land as her friend and also foe. She was grateful for every feather and stone a child had brought her as proof of their turning from street kids and thieves into careful individuals, able to see treasures where none had been before, and all this knowledge of a life beautifully and humbly lived was there alongside Peter on that hillside. He poured the ashes, not scattered, but poured into a neat little cone on the ground and looked at this his friend, so tiny there, going back to the ground, barely even the same weight as she had been when she arrived, and he sensed an aura an awe-ra so immense. It felt like Margaret stood by him, no longer the birdlike stick she had become in her latter years but this time as a strong, tall personality towering over 'her' hill. The view that had been hers from her tumbledown little cottage, the one that was now owned by Peter. Not of his asking but of her giving, in the same way as she had given her whole life for this moment, this new Margaret, smelling of roses, risen herself, and due to start her next adventure.

Margaret, Oh! that we could be as you were, unhurried by modern living, unruffled by others' demands, just decent and caring and clever beyond doubt. Your inner knowing, striding manfully in womanhood to this potent end. Peter felt this, saw it in his mind's eye and cried a tear, not of sadness but of depth, for never had he been party to such a sense of future as now and never would he be exactly the same Peter from that moment on. Margaret affecting him from her realm even now. He smiled, turned and left the little cone of Margaret essence, a wiser man himself.

Meanwhile, the residue of the explosive froth, no longer pent up and pressured, quiet now, just being. There in the cool dampness, waiting. Zofia, let us give a name to the new form this atom of goo has helped create. One part that peeled its way into the world, defied the odds of life turning back on itself in a cul-de-sac of evolution, survived the journey out of the hold of a ship and onwards throughout the country, this tiny part refusing to be halted in its tracks by the ravages of disinfectant. Unlike some, who appear to try so hard, do their best, get so far, only to be cut off in their prime. This small part, tiny Zofia's-worth of goo, a small bit has eschewed the everyday fate of her fellows and come out, not entirely unscathed but changed, using the heat of scathment to better herself, shape shift, join forces with another strength having squeezed out of the grip that was the norm signalling the end, the demise of the common parts of goo. Peter's farm is safe from that particular encroachment. Phew! Let normal life reign again, the postman return as a visitor and deliveries be a part of everyday life. This will happen soon, once the wider scourge has done and the regulations lifted.

Meanwhile, Zofia is resting, her next trick up her sleeve. Still holding that memory of reproduction handed over from the second splitting in the hold of the ship, now adding yet another trick of evolution to her list. Shape shifting, changing, slightly mutating, just enough to get by in a scrape, a situation where others could not survive, straining, paining perhaps, to rebirth. Her moves being the achievements of her race, a new race not yet written in the history books because she is yet unknown. This is a race to come, part of the future flowering in a land where some has gone extinct, has already played its part in transporting this portion of Zofia into her rightful place. She is not only changed but also joined, moved on from a single type of life to open the way for another, already experienced in blending and making new substances to test the world and enhance. Zofia, a fitting name, to encompass this duo become one, a new life and sex for this emergent microorganism. What job will you fulfil in the future on this farm? The effort of striving in your nature now, joined seamlessly, balanced, with another, this common hydrogen, whose strivings and achievements are evident all around, in air and water and solid state, mixed to make our everyday life. Hydrogen enmeshed in common things, taken for granted, stepped on, over and within us every day. The magic of chemistry all around us. Did one part of goo plus hydrogen make chemistry and out of that, the partnership of Zofia is born, ready to move again in a world open to new ideas of all kinds, always? She is here, part of Peter's farm, a new part, waiting to see if she can find another forward move for her brand new race. She is the animal that trekked its way out of the desert of Africa into a new habitat and survived, the animal that found itself floating on an island continent and made a new design for itself, like the marsupials of the Antipodes, different, unique to their continent but showing still the beginnings like every other earthbound creature.

The old goo, no longer potent, killed off by treatment, consistent hammering at the edges of its evolving force, will soon be gone. The struggle is uneven, the disinfectant will win this one out. Let Zofia through. She is different, she showed skills beyond the average of her race's beginnings. Is she the clever one? Does she hold the intelligence of adaptability in her memory now? What will she think of next? Can we give this little one that trait, intelligence? Does she know what she has done, or is it the striving an instinct for Life's own longing for itself? Shall the gift of the word, intelligence, be tempered, taken down just a notch to instinct? Is instinct where we have all grown out of? The strong instinct to save our young, protect our babies, nurture and teach, pass on our learnings. Instinct to suckle, to feed, to show love, like Peter's new cow/calf, day/night system is allowing – using instinct and Peter's intelligence as the forward plan. Is Peter making chemistry at another scale? Scale! We have been here before!

Think of the calf, knowing to track around his mother's side to seek out the life-giving teat in the dark recesses of her warm under flank? The cow, instinct to lick and tend that calf, her newborn, who, without this mother's protection and food would be cold and hungry, not long for the world. How does this work? When does intelligence become instinct? For Zofia, she changes, that is the same as intelligence, but if she can pass that trait to her future generations for them is it instinct?

Downgraded once it becomes easy, intelligence when it is from straining for the new. In straining and effort new knowledge is gained. And what do we do, as a race, human race? Are we learning, evolving, passing on intelligent information to our future generations so it can become instinct in them and free them up to move, to take the next step, to move beyond the limitation of their parents? Have you taught that to your children? Peter is learning, he is finding a new place within him where his ideas are HIS ideas. He has done with that cul-de-sac, the blind following of others' grandiose schemes that spill him and his small farm beyond the scale he is happy to work in. He wants to know his animals well, to see them perform their instincts in front of him, to experience the beauty and intelligence of his cows caring for their young and be a whole part of it. He is at one with his animals, sharing in their grief as it was, and now desiring to share in their joy. What better sight than a field where mothers munch and chew and cud their way through the day and their calves, in gangs, form friendships and mock battles and run races and love their lives. He is happy to forgo the worries and stress of the subsidy for this.

For him this is evolution on his farm, the pain he had to go through to change, to shape shift, to adapt and squeeze his way out of the scalding searing heat of his aching heart. He made sideways steps to avoid the disintegration of his whole livelihood in the disinfectant of false direction. A disinfectant willing to scour out and away the small farms in our midst, making way only for the oversized, but Peter could see down that route, see that this is a cul-de-sac, an impossible growth pattern. The sterile disinfectant of off-farm advice and subsidy, devoid of feeling, burning away the possibility of sustainability. Not for growth at all costs, for that will in the end cost all, but for a standing still, a making the best of now, finding out what strengths there lie in resting up for a bit, waiting, finding the way forward with new tools, perhaps even tools that are not yet completely evolved. Those coming into being, new, in scale with what is possible. They are there. New ideas are always there, coalescing in the minds of those who will open their minds and let them in.

Rest up, open your mind, let in the new. Zofia is.

Chapter 15

*Creativity and innovation is the birthright
of every nation – Peter taps this fertile vein,
again, again, again, again.*

Now a shift came over Peter in his half waking state. Early morning routine had been moved slightly forward so that instead of the rasping 4a.m. call he had one more pleasant hour of reverie to pull through before wakeful consciousness tugged him into the everyday world. Years, longer than he could easily count, of 4a.m. waking were ingrained in his physicality; hence his body stirring early, drawing closer to the surface yet there was not the last urgency of the shrill alarm to jolt him, jar him out of his supine position.

He lay on his back, relaxed, aware, but just in that zone where the feeling in his body had not returned. He was being Peter but without the attachment of Peter's bodily sensations. This was the most relaxed yet conscious he could be and he loved it. He knew from past experimentation that staying completely still he could imagine that he had handed over his body weight to something so large, so flat, so expansive that he was spread out like a puddle in the sunlight and he soaked up that warmth gratefully. This was where his reverie was best received; lately he had awarded himself this time for thinking, or musing on gentle subjects. Peter's subjects were always gentle, he was a gentle man. Caring and open to change these days. He felt like he had broken the back of the old habits and he laughed at them when they returned like an old friend, but one who was still stuck with schoolboy humour and habits, when he had grown up, grown into himself, accepted the responsibility of family life and able and capable of putting others before his own selfish wishes. Peter's family substitute was the farm, the animals, the fields and fences and more importantly the natural lives that all this supported. All this came under the umbrella of family for our Peter. He would gladly have also accepted wife and child, but that was out of his control and weeping over old hurts was no longer in Peter's armoury of self-supporting tools. No crutches here, only a stout stick for striding forward, a stout stick to use to test the ground before taking a step blindly. This sensible man had a good brain, a rounded attitude and a handsome rugged appearance now that shone with the changes he had made within. The stuttering, weeping, cowed, stooped Peter of yesteryear firmly brought under control by this the new man. He shone, like the sun that was rising behind the curtains of his meagre bedroom.

A rising energy began in Peter's being, he was learning about his connectivity to the world and he loved it. Always he had known that he and animals were One at some level. He had spent too many hours with these, his darling beasts, to doubt that. There was an unspoken communication in the milking parlour, in the field and in the sheds. They would move around each other with ease and acceptance of their place together in this world. An acceptance of his help at hand with a difficult calving or of water pollution. Once there had been a leak at a trough on a remote part of the farm. Peter had not spotted this quickly, he was too preoccupied with work closer to home and the cattle had taken to drinking where they could. A tiny stream, more of a seasonal ditch, had been flowing at the time and these girls, thirsty from giving of their morning milk had used this to drink from. Unease in the herd about the disappointment of seeking first at a dry trough and then having to search out this substandard water had somehow been alerted to Peter. His sensibilities around his animals were up, alerted, touched in an uncanny way. He chose to leave his work and wander through the fields checking fences and gateways – the unease had no specific enquiry attached but drew him positively towards where the cows were grazing that day. Immediately he could see the problem, hoof marks struggling in the ditch were the sign. Why would the animals bother to put themselves through such an exercise? And then it twigged, dropped into place like a perfect piece of jigsaw. Water, there were no cows at the trough. They had given up with that route and changed their habit. He was able then to attend to the problem, a practical problem to solve, that was Peter's forte. Soon he had the water flowing, rushing to fill the trough again, clean fresh water. He called his cows with his special 'coomaan' shout. They responded immediately and all was well before any significant problems occurred. The ditch was re-fenced and the cows drank deeply, washing any dirt from their throats and filling their capacious guts again, ready to refill the udder that was the life-giving stuff of this farm.

On the farm a strange transformation was taking place, Peter, our man, was clearing his clouds of doubt and fear, passing off old slights and taking on new challenges willingly. Yes, he had relaxed into this new life.

Coping alone for several years had taken its toll and gradually the knots in his stomach and tightness in his neck had become his normal way of working. This book, Margaret's gift to him, was helping him to come to terms with old hurts and put them away beyond the reach of his emotions. It was not that he was hypnotising himself into forgetting, but that the memories had been assigned their proper place in history and the issues surrounding them were no longer the emotional tug-of-war he used to experience. He had mistaken 'being in a state of worry', for caring, when he should have been either resolving the problem, if he could – like he had by bravely looking into the family farm affair – or, coming to terms with his part in 'the incident', a real low point in his life. New patterns of thought gradually emerged from below the layer of habitual glumness and even he recognised the carefree Peter of his youth appearing from time to time. Peter began to bother to go out more often and at first he felt shy, as if he had little to offer but as time and familiarity took over, his demeanour changed and he was relaxed in the company of his fellow farming friends. No group is an island and other faces emerged, non-farming folk who lived in and around his area with whom he thought he had little in common, suddenly became interesting to be around. It was refreshing to hear others' opinions and even refreshing to find that he didn't agree but still could enjoy the company and the debate. Peter, you changed man, almost human again, and why?

Can we put it down to the relationship Peter was unwittingly developing with his smaller parts? They were there for all the traumas and while they could never talk to Peter, they sure could make him jump. The realisation that he had actually still been working for his grandmother, even when she no longer required it was not fair to her memory. In her day, Grandmother had herself been an innovative farmer, she had scrimped and saved and improved to the best of her ability and of her time. Peter was pushing at the boundaries of his time now – taking these memories and putting them to good use or else in the scrapbook of his mind, pasted in by his firm hand to be opened and looked at when he chose rather than when they happened to float to the fore. OK, he was still caught out. Who flagged up the last disaster also had to put it back to bed. Peter was asserting himself to the most important and prescient person in his life, Himself, and he loved it. He loved to catch himself out, sliding down into the easy downward spiral of the blame culture; well weather, well money, well get your act together Peter would say to himself. To himself? Which bit? His atoms affecting his humour, his health, physical and mental – better clean them right up.

Peter, at first, was not sure how to cope with his new situation. He felt the need for change and had actually made many changes on the farm, but it was this inner work that was so new to him. He had not even realised before just what a world of understanding he was couched in, all his stuff had been automatic, grown slowly out of his love for the animals, his basic human need to see things well cared for. He may no longer be a husband to the mother of his distant child but he understood better than ever what the term husbandry meant in the farming sense and the responsibility it gave him. More than ever his desire was for a quiet, clean existence. One where his contribution, whatever it was, seen or unseen by others felt like it was building on the positivity of the general flow of the planet. He had been there, been joined, flowed as Reality flowed, not inside his head but inside the tiniest portion of this surrounding world where there flowed yet another world, desperate to contribute, desperate to assist, offer from afar, yet near.

Oh my, the World of Paradox, where the largest space was contained within the smallest place. The atom, his tiny friend who understood him, stood under – which was it? Impossible to pin down yet so, so real to this new Peter, the guy happy to put forward his ideas in a crowded room, the shy boy grown up, taken in hand by himself, rounded and grounded by the physical sensible work he attended to in the everyday world, was now party to the ideas and forces of a world so large and full and soft and gracious and powerful that he stood in awe of it and could explain it to no one. He had no one to explain it to anyway, he still lived his solitary existence on the farm, attending daily to his duties, always caring, he had also become loving. Not soppy or stupid, far too much common sense ran through this man's brain and life for that, but loving in a different way, possibly respectful describes it better. It was a projected love. It appeared before him in the place where he would do his next spell of work. It floated before him as intention to do the very best he could and he thought it carefully through too. He was still a farmer, now he kept his beloved calves, and they kept their beloved mothers and they all embraced the new-found peace on the farm. The inevitable day of market, or a private sale happened. He thanked the cattle for their part and sent them onwards, hoping that their fate would be kindly, but also accepting it was now out of his hands into the hands of those further down the chain. He hoped the gentle aura of his cattle and quality of their gifts, be it for milk or beef would stand out and a fair exchange made. That was the deal he made with them, his part in the mutual exchange made. He now moved on to the next task in hand, happier and guilt free.

Monday morning had brought great changes to Peter's farm life. His whole demeanour had changed for the better, with head lifted high, a spring in his step and the air of a man on a mission he marched down to the cowshed. In there he viewed his treasured animals. He held a plan in his mind, and a tape measure in his pocket. This plan was one that had come to him whilst hanging on in the special place that he could now retreat to at will. This achievement had not come about lightly or easily, months of patient practice brought his mental capacity to a new level, transcending any other he had ever experienced but this was such a tiny thing in some respects and huge at the same time. He had achieved a change of attitude! To what? Well, to everything. He had worked hard to set his finances in order, scaled down on expenses, keeping just the equipment he needed for a comfortable and efficient working life. Work was his life, farming had always been his life, all he had ever desired to do or be and he had stuck at it. Very nearly, a few times, he had been on the verge of giving up, throwing in the towel, but it is not so easy when your responsibilities revolve around other lives counting on you for their food, water and shelter. The very act of administering these basic needs had pulled him through. He recognised that love and gratitude from these animals had also been his fodder, not in a literal sense, but tending the cows, the calves and even the wild farm cats, seeing their reaction to being satisfied, watered and bedded down. The contented rhythm of cudding jaws, the gloop of the next cud as it rises in the neck, that was his succour. Wordless but deep contentment, satisfaction, the herd balanced with young and old at peace in each other's company. Here was the place that Peter sought recreation, his work became his recreation in a positive and literal manner. This man's stature powered that unspoken grid around him. He shone, a man in his element, and it was reciprocal.

Take a deep, deep breath and enter into the shining soul that is Peter's new attitude. Let us compare to the man he was – the chap whose downtrodden existence seemed to drag him through tasks that he hated; ripping away the child from the mother – acting unnaturally for such a gentle man, feeding the substandard feed to these babies, knowing they deserved better but unable to be the one who turned the tide, for the tide had hold of him, tossing and turning itself every which way but sense, in his mind. All he could do was to rise momentarily to the surface of this foaming froth of a sea that his life had become and take a hasty breath before being dragged down back to the rasping bottom of the ocean of gloom, of despair, the pits. His raw soul scraped painfully along the bottom, pulling all his joy, his vision for future away from him, putting him in the position of working just for survival of the moment. That is where Peter had come from, and it had hurt... badly.

The next part of the story comes from Peter's heart, which is singing with joy. He can see a way out of his position of loneliness on the farm. He is to offer his new-found friend, Cheese Lady, some room on the farm. The parlour, already kitted up as a food grade area was now too large. He could shrink the milking areas easily and allow her to be there. It can be a temporary arrangement, just to get her going. Then his milk market was also assured. He would have company and they could discuss where the arrangement went after a trial period, all very sensible and mutually beneficial. Now all he had to do was speak to her and discover her reaction.

Peter was entering another stage of his life. He felt it in everything he did, as if there was more purpose than just 'getting by' which is what his former incarnation had felt like. His understanding of his cattle had deepened now they were able to fully express themselves around their family unit. Cows and calves together, a family with interactions and games and tired calves seeking out their mothers for a drink and a lick of comfort before being led to a safe sleeping area, hidden if possible from general view but with mum's eye just 'on guard' at all times. Sometimes older siblings would be allowed to take charge and mothers would go off together, just like humans might like some time away from children's hankerings and take a break, to return refreshed, ready for another round of child care. Peter wished he could have had the bull in there too, but this was a step too far for this scheme of his. He was still dependent on milk as his livelihood even if he had almost halved production from the girls on his patch.

The day/night cow/calf regime was working so

well, he hardly ever had any of the everyday ailments. Mastitis and foot problems had reduced. Certainly the trauma of separation was gone. There were still a few logistical problems and sometimes calves disobeyed orders by getting back with mum at night but this he forgave generously, knowing that even in this system he had disturbed the natural order of things. What was excellent though was the fun he had seeing calves out at play. Because he had been giving up his calves at such a young age, and always so dismally, and he was sure the calves felt it too, they had both missed out on this joy. Now, high tails and running like little personal cowboy film shows, they raced and rushed and mooed their way about the place, jostling and head butting in mock fights and championships. That this had been denied him, a farmer through and through, he knew now why he did love this job, exactly for these reasons. The long days and short nights were worth every bit of loss of sleep and windy, rainy day that he had ever lived.

He thanked himself for daring to change and then realised he had not dared. It was a step he had to take. Going further down the other route may have been his total undoing – and he would not have been the first. Farming was known to be one of the most dangerous professions, accidents with machinery was one side of it, and suicides the other. He had been lucky with the machinery so far, but he felt as if he had come close to thoughts too dangerous to even contemplate. It was, in fact, his weekly visit to his friend Margaret that had brought him the little light every week that kept him going. Margaret, thank you, thank you; Peter felt her beside him briefly as he thought of her. Her strength of character and goodness rubbing off on him still, even though no physical part of her graced this world anymore. It was not a memory of Margaret he experienced. It was Margaret, there beside him, also admiring the view. Calves having fun.

Chapter 16

A rite of passage, dark days behind – new ventures
with an open mind where 'possible' is always signed.

Here we have Peter, head in hands and studying the plans in front of him. He has committed to changing his old dairy into a new and different kind of food room and needs to work out where he can reuse what is there and still come up to scratch for his new partner as well as satisfying his need to spend as little as possible. He wants to make a useful area, easy to rearrange because he understands how a business has to change and grow and adjust as time goes along. The dairy walls and floor are still good but there has to be provision for different electrical equipment and standing room for workers carrying and stretching and shifting vats of milk around. Milk is heavy and slops about, smooth running wheels must roll freely for difficult manoeuvres. At least he has now found an outlet for his milk. It is such a wonderful feeling to know where his farm produce is going. He always felt so remote from all parts of his business. He saw calves go off in one direction, out of his hands and out of his ken and the milk lorry trundling off with the milk, straight to another farm to add into the huge container. There was no real pride in that. The quality, although coming back to him as a readout on a sheet of paper, did not really register. Whereas now, it would be imperative that the quality was excellent and consistent and even more importantly he had someone who was interested in his production methods to talk to. Someone who may not have a huge knowledge as yet but did have a sparkle in her eye and a keenness to learn and know and understand. He was so happy to be onto a new project. It was understood to be a temporary measure until a suitable food unit could be found, hence the need to keep costs to a minimum, but Peter was keen to be helpful since it suited him to be able to sell his milk to the Cheese Lady, as he had dubbed her in his mind, and the parlour already achieved most of the criteria for hygiene and was now oversized for his reduced milking herd. This project taxed his brain and stretched his thoughts away from the usual tracks. It was refreshing and he looked forward to discussing how to get the show on the road as soon as possible.

Peter, our man of the moment, is fully occupied with a task. Concentration furrows his brow, a smeary hand wiping away the sweat of deep thought.

Beside him one of the farm cats comes for a comfort and a reminder that her food dish is empty. A natural movement, automatic in its sincerity, our man swipes his whole large, mucky hand down the length of the cat, head to tip of tail. Registering in that movement that Cat is not forgotten but also not quite top of the list at this moment. Another unspoken but very real cross species communication takes place on this magical farm where few words are spoken but many sentiments conveyed. Are we so clever in our everyday skills at communication? Possibly not, unless glum faces, staring into impersonal screens are actually telling us the story of the state of mind of the general population. Cat understands that she has her message through, glances at the as yet unfilled bowl and goes to amuse herself elsewhere, convinced that the food will arrive soon enough.

The cattle similarly speak to Peter; they convey through movement and demeanour their mood of the moment. Huge pregnant sides, lifted high on one side make lying discomfort obvious when deep rasping breath escapes from the cow nose and throat. Heaving herself to her feet, tell-tale shifts in udder and vulva qualities signal a near birth. Peter is aware of all of this as second nature. It is his job to be not just guardian of the bank balance but also the guardian of the well-being of these creatures. That is his job and he loves it with a love that extends beyond a 9 to 5 commitment for a 'fair' wage or an 'entitled' feel that he is worth more than a fellow worker through rank or birth. Peter does not place himself either above or below these animals he cares for. He is 'at one' with them. His recognition of their place in his world is one on a level playing field; he rather envies them their lives without interference from their fellow species in unwanted areas. A cow would never ask another to wear ear tags, she already knows and understands who her fellow cow is. A cat doesn't need the deeds to her house, she marks her territory with scent and with stand offish night time warning calls before giving in or fighting her corner. Peter has dealt with the ear tags, for one of his fellow species who will never meet his cows nor care which ones are sluggish, which loving and which curious, exactly how he takes their differences into consideration, and the cat did not help him when he had to pore over the farm deeds with family members' fortunes in mind. Fortunately that affair had gone smoothly without posturing or name calling – in other families it would not be resolved so easily.

Peter, still smeary, goes indoors for a cup of tea to wash the dust from his throat, and a good lathery face and hand wash before the next task is upon him. He has not forgotten Cat whose bowl was filled, in a passing gesture, with a splosh of milk. Raw unadulterated milk, just like every calf should drink. Milk full of natural antibodies, vitamins and minerals, with a depth to it beyond the mere substance. It conveyed the love of a cow to her calf. Milk floated this small farm in bank and bucket. Milk was the life-giving force of the calves and the humans that used it as their currency. Milk, given so many jobs to do other than its natural intended one, yet somehow undervalued, underused by the supermarkets for what it really stands – Life Giving Substance. Why? Why? Oh why does it have to be handed to the public in such a wrecked state, so it is hardly recognisable from the stream of white, frothy life-giving stuff of ages. Plasticised, torn apart, heated, cooled, diminished in physicality and stature, sent swooping down the chart of the 50 best loved foods. Overtaken by brand and biscuit and beer and bullshit, when once it was handed to each child every day as a panacea to keep teeth and bones healthy, feed without fattening and ensure each child's little working brain could tick its way towards the end of lesson bell. When did the bottom fall out of the common sense of food?

Be drawn into this bowl as Cat, neat white paws tucked in under her chest, leans over, pink tongue, raspy pink tongue lap, lap, lapping, sending rhythmic little ripples through the milk, obvious from the circular pattern upon the surface of the decreasing amount of milk in front of her. Draw forward dear reader and watch as ripples break and build in this tiny pond, replicating the waves on a sea or lake, exactly the same patterns forming in miniature here as would and are forming all over our known universe. No one and nothing escapes this phenomenon, the wave makers. Here Cat is the wave machine. Where do you make waves in your life? Peter has taken his life in hand, he made waves in the office of 'they money men'. He withdrew. He melted out from underneath their clasp, not entirely, but in such a manner as to shock them. Their whole existences revolve around looking for deals. Their whole existences skim around in the human made world of subsidy and deal, and billions in this pot and applying for millions in another pot. They slither among the rules and regulations, with understanding the ways round the loopholes and it takes them all their time to keep up with this changing sea. A raft of legislation never perfect, unable to be perfect because one size does not fit all, and the satisfied in this corner register their disbelief if the dissatisfied in another part complain, rock the boat, find a strong voice to put forward a valid argument, an opposing raft of reason, some evidence for them that requires the whole structure to reform. While the other Peters of this farming world must conform, conform, conform as the waves of legislation and government splash over their heads, sweeping the flotsam and jetsam of the non-trending moment to the side, to smash to pieces on the rocks or be left high and dry like the little piece of sad debris abandoned in the now empty cat bowl. The cat, satisfied, walks away still licking her lips and doing that very cat thing of stretching each limb whilst on the move, unperturbed by anyone else in her species. Time for a pleasant nap.

Peter is in a turmoil of excitement, he has built the internal partition walls and covered them with a washable parlour board. He wants to know from Cheese Lady where she would like shelves. Ideally she will have a stack of shelves on wheels, but until she gets the dimensions of her more permanent unit she does not want to commit her money so Peter is stepping in and making some interim ones. He is enjoying himself, being creative and helpful and having this new-found companion as well as his happy herd. Life at last is good, just as it should be for a man so talented and loving and caring. Is that not what all our lives should be about? Can we use our talents to best advantage for more than just ourselves, bring some help and joy to others too? This was a two way street, Cheese Lady with her idea, her blank canvas, Peter with milk to sell. She was intrigued and grateful at how Peter could just magic up a perfect room for her to get her experimental station on the go. Her timescale had been pretty woolly. All she knew was that she could not possibly go back to the grind that her old life had become and that the meditation of mixing, stirring and cutting cheese was the direction she was destined to go in.

Magic cheese, choosing its own personality from the ingredients. She did not know or understand this in person as yet but her teacher had fired her enthusiasm and as a wine taster can suck out of the air, the nuances of a fine wine so she, Peter's Cheese Lady, was determined that her cheese would have its own character. This was why she was so keen to find a source of milk that came from a farm with distinction. Her idea of distinction had been in the land. Would it be through the chalkiness of the ground or the clay? Is that where her sense of 'terroir' would come from? Instead, she found the distinction in the manner that Peter kept his cows. It was the gentleness of his system, but more so the personality of the cows, their manner and demeanour that would show in the character of the cheese. She was not a farmer, did not understand animals like Peter did. She could not read the small signs and may not have picked up on the signals that Peter did, but she could sense the peace and calm and fun of these animals and once Peter began to talk about them, knowing each cow, calf and sisterhood there on his patch, that was where her feeling for distinction came in. This was something unique, and she was sure that her cheese would show this distinction in the end. As yet unmade, the cheese-to-be was already glowing and attracting good attention from another source. There was a fire in her eye for her burgeoning career and in Peter's eye a sparkle that had not been there just twelve months before.

It was dark before Peter had finished the rounds of his dear animals; he never hurried this last evening job. There was no one at home to hurry back to and these animals, the ones who afforded his lifestyle as well as his full freezer, allowed him to stay in this job that he loved. Above all else they were the ones where his best quality of solace came from. He had had his sad times, had been through some terrifying internal journeys but also he was so very proud of the fact that he had come through all that because of his deep inner knowledge that this job, farming, was for him. He considered it his vocation, an old-fashioned term in these days of atheism or agnosticism, not that he really understood what either of those words meant. Grandmother had been a church goer; he had given that up as soon as his opinion was considered valid in the household. His Sunday mornings had been better spent, he felt, in the cathedral of the open countryside, often with one or two, or a gang of the lads from the village. Sometimes Margaret's boys would join in the roaming and there his adventures and fun and tree climbing and bog hopping and jumping brooks and streams filled him with happiness and helped his soul to sing. The dour serious sermons a thing of his past. Free, just for a while until adulthood caught up with him and responsibilities piled up, as if his ribbon through life, so joyful, free in the breeze as a youngster got snagged up in the trials and tribulations of living.

The pregnancy, not planned and a shock, but one that Peter soon hove to with, and accepted gracefully as his responsibility. Worse, the short episode following that where he bonded with his child, but drifted apart from her mother, sometimes jagged separation cut him, the gentle soul of Peter ripped and pained by this tearing wrench, losing the child so firmly integrated into his heart. But that was then and he had plenty of other problems to solve. Grandmother's slow demise, where her helping hands became weaker, although her mind, conversation and ideas were his way through at times. The sadness after she was gone, when he struggled with his conscience about the farm, family obligations and a heavy blanket of cloud over all of that. It started before Grandmother died. They had both been in agreement to join with the subsidy payments then on offer, but it felt as if gradually the string was pulled ever tighter, the restrictions and obligations from his side more uneven. What had, at first, looked like a healthy lifeline became a snare, catching the smaller fish and putting them to one side, to be knocked off one by one as if they counted for nothing. Much easier to work from the handout end with a few big farms employing permanent office staff, than to be mithering on with the small fry. Loneliness kicked in hard after the grandmother thing and compounded his feelings of hopelessness. Masculine training, although never spoken out loud, was in the air all around in his growing up years and was a wall he had learnt to remove, brick by painful brick. Margaret was the only one where those rules did not apply and her genuine level playing field before and after her death was what braced him, buttressed him against his own depression and linked him to his other side, the one where Hope was the biggest draw and the knowledge rising from his deepest parts made him wonder at his stubbornness to keep on keeping on through the darkest of times, pull himself through on the steady cogs of animal feed times and milking parlour routine.

My, how he had struggled to keep an even keel, there were tears, and snot and blind stumblings and mistakes and fear and periods of what felt like endless grief to push past, kick his way through. Never had he felt determination like he had in those hardest of times, and then breakthrough! His tiny triumph with the hare, not even knowing the outcome, just the feeling, snatching himself and the hare from the jaws of death and destruction, but not even caring in that moment whether he lived or died. He lived, and his friend, the driver, friend of that moment had been there stomping on that brake for him, letting him through as well as the leveret. Just in that moment he triumphed and that turned around the whole mood of the farm. His farm, strength given to find this out, his farm? This was the turning point, he looked, he took the situation in hand and good surprises came around each corner.

Was it luck? Or did Peter drive this with his determination to hang on when there could have been a different option? What do you think? When The Voice came to Peter's aid, Peter was down, driven down to his last gram of energy and there he asked for help. The help came from an unusual source, not physical but energetic. It gave him a new perspective where the hill to climb seemed doable. Turning points are like that, outwardly nothing changes except the orientation. Spin yourself around, then the climb is in a different direction, the slope a little less steep and the rewards quicker to arrive. Peter did that, followed his inner desire, despite odds stacked against him and he found his turning point. He put in the work to change. The effort of staying in the bad and hurtful place was just as much of a struggle as taking on the new. He dared to change and look at his outcome. He threw away the subsidy because he had looked into the difficult family fearful place and been given a chance. He changed the farm, rearranged his life around the new circumstances and became light-hearted again.

Nothing could be as bad as being down there on the bottom, very nearly hoisted permanently over the edge.

Buoyed with new energy, he floated, rose just a little and saw another horizon to conquer. It did not happen in a day. This was not an unrealistic lottery winning shock of a rise, but studied, hand over hand he heaved himself upwards. He tackled loneliness by going out, he chose to go among fellow farmers, and met others, non-farming folk. It did not solve his loneliness on the farm – perhaps that is for another story – but he made the effort, and boy, that was an effort. Peter's memory of difficult times in a crowd at market still clung a little, he was not sure how he could manage it, but the strength was there when he needed it. Over time, he found friendships, the awkwardness gone, he could converse and meld into the crowd. Like his tiny atom friend, the ones he did not even know were with him on their own turn of the dice, or swing of the pendulum, he became more whole by being one amongst many, single, but one of a crowd. Mankind, there to support each other, not to take advantage of the weakest. Those days of evolution are over for humankind, we are onto the next phase. We feel it in the air around us but do we respond? In words, yes. We look after our elderly and disadvantaged; lip service perhaps, we could be doing it better. Like Peter's farm is coming through a revolution of his making, but with help from within, from his Ideas Place, good ideas are there for all of us if we will but stop long enough to allow them to surface. Humankind, each single one of us, in a crowd can rise and pull up all those around us. Beautiful world, cathedral for our development, playground for our experiments – let us make them work.

It is the end of a busy day, all the animals are neatly wrapped up for the evening. Some in a cosy byre, some still in a dry, high field and others mooching in a barn. Peter in his chair beside the wood burner, an open book in his hand, happy that he has done his best by the creatures under his care. There will be another day, another whole round of the routine, more surprises to deal with and problems to contend with but that's what makes this life such fun. There will be time to lean on the gate and stare, just stare at the newborns, admire and love them, grateful for their part on his watch. My, he was tired, but happily so. Food in his belly, clean, dry, warm bed to sleep in. What more can a man desire? Well, possibly there is something missing but that is a problem to solve another day, perhaps even another story. In the meantime, enjoying the contentment of work well done, a clear conscience and a good sleep to come was all that he needed for today.

You have come a long way, my man. You now row your own boat too, you plough your own furrow and like Margaret before you, you are destined for Higher Things. Yawning, Peter closed his book and placed it on the table, at last we see the title, Space for Farming.

Epilogue

The scales we deal with, large and small,
have further meaning for us all.

The small things in life are the important ones, just catching up with friends and family when it is needed gives much succour but to have this removed from your life because of circumstance is a trial not many can bear. Replacing this lost and missing love is possible by working with animals close to your heart. Peter found this out, in fact his love was huge, he could easily have shared it all around but his fortunes had shrunk in that area and he had to make do with what hand he had been dealt. A missing wife and child, few family, none really close by, his good friend Margaret and Grandmother gone to their resting places and him, there on his little farm, probably happier than he had been for a long time but lonely for the companionship of his own species. His sensibilities were acute enough to be able to form good relationships with his farm animals, they all walked a steady path nowadays and Dog had brought smiles into the farmyard. Man's first true animal friend, bred to be useful and loyal and fun, and Dog lived up to his ancestry. Cat also held her place in Peter's heart, she and her friends used the house as a resting place during the day and her warmth and soft fur comforted Peter as she purred whilst being stroked, contented to allow this closeness – on her own terms – and attend to nocturnal duties. But there were others who tugged at Peter's heart strings now, he loved his cows and he had the calves back in the fold. This time he was not needed to feed milk from a bottle or mimic the long rasping licks of a mother cow, that was all in place and the correct being was on the job, on the case. He could watch though and enjoy the loving spectacle from close up.

The cow conversation from mother to calf began well before birth and every calf understood the vibration of his mother's lowing – field games with other calves were comical and speedy hightailing over the fields, practising their own strange baby bellows brought more smiles, but it was the peacefulness that Peter enjoyed, even in the rushing stampede of calf exercise and the mad flurry of a crazy dog five minute's madness, the whole farm had an air of calm and order. This re-establishment of order had returned Peter to the place he had been in when he was younger, when Grandmother had been fit and well and in charge of the farm and although they were never well off, there had been a settled feeling of earnings being fair, with enough to put towards the ongoing repairs and small improvements needed to keep up with the times. At that time Peter did not feel the burden of responsibility, his was to attend to the work, and decisions, although talked through, ultimately were made from Grandmother's side. He had been happy then and there was time between the two workers to keep a tidy ship, then just gradually the slippage had started, but we know all this, it is what the story has been about.

Peter had regained his equilibrium, caught up with the work, was loving the happiness he could sense in his animals and had shot well past the place on the farm wellbeing chart that he had expected. He mused about this from time to time and did his best to work out what exactly had happened to change his fortunes around. It was hard to put an exact finger on it. Was it the elusive place in his mind where he could hold the peace and calm, or the confidence held within him now that all was well in his world because he was willing to work towards it? He was enjoying his excitement at having made a different system of animal keeping work, and the way his fortune had granted him the opportunity to help someone at the same time as securing his income. He could see how this cheese business was totally able to thrive; the commercial world was opening to high-class small-scale businesses too. He was building a working partnership with Cheese Lady. They agreed to understand each other's world of work more thoroughly. Each would give time to work and watch, make this cheesemaking business more holistic and support each other through the inevitable teething problems to come. She understood business, her old life had sickened her of it and she was determined that a business under her charge would be different. Peter understood farming and had also been sickened by his experiences. They made a pact; change for the better would come their way. These were two realistic grown-ups joining forces and becoming greater than the sum of their parts.

Soon the initial incarnation of the goo would be gone, conquered by government legislation, disinfectant and hours of extra work and vigilance by farmers. What is left is new, inexperienced and fearlessly willing to try every avenue afforded by the intelligence and instinct driving Zofia, a pairing as yet unfulfilled in its mission – a story yet to be told!

Peter has another string to his bow too. The gift

from Margaret, a badly bashed up dwelling yet to bring rewards and security, but that is also for another story.

But how had this happened? There was in this new-found peacefulness also another kind of substance, the air felt thick with it, coming round the corners a new kind of light appeared to shine. Peter felt it and could not explain it. He felt as if it was something that had the possibility of being there all the time but had to be tuned into, like happiness or sadness or joy or disappointment. All these real yet not quite tangible emotions are there hanging in the ether just waiting to be tapped into, wrong to say they are within us, no, they exist outside us and we tune into them and light them up or dull them down depending on the person in charge of the switch. An actor does it, they inhabit their character well enough to switch into the mood necessary to make the character work, be believable. The ham actor squeezes it out from within and it is a thin playing of the emotion. The good actor picks up on the vibration of the scene because all possibilities are there all of the time for all of us. These were the thoughts that Peter wrestled with as he went about his quiet days.

His farm hung with expectation that all was well,

and problems could and would be resolved. Solutions were delivered from without Peter's world. Ironically they arrived because Peter had changed himself from someone relying on flimsy man-made hopes and dead end deals, to a man of courage with a willingness to make his own changes, to implement ideas that had come to him from deep within. He had stirred the Stuff of Creativity and it responded. Creative ideas born of a frustration and need for change that had him teetering on the edge of a situation so severe that his severance from it had to come one way or another and the animals had helped just by being there, needing him to fulfil his part of the bargain. But it was more than that, as Peter thought about his changes and the ones that had come about, the more he felt as if he had found the switch and been the switch at the same time, and good old Paradox was there too, this tiny Noplace, that impossible reference point on the seesaw of Life, where his ideas came from, affected this outer place where he lived and worked, and this outer place was huge. It went beyond the hedges of his farm, now secure and tidy, beyond the high hill where he had left that last grainy portion of his wonderful friend Margaret and beyond county, country and beyond again into the skies and on again beyond the atmosphere and the moon and even beyond his sun and on and on into that wide night time firmament, studded with an array of stars, knowing also that those stars were just the few visible to his wondering eyes and that even more lay beyond and he felt Connected. No longer the inward looking cringing cold sweat of a man but one whose turned round life made him expansive and as he thought these things his mood, in response, felt gladness and tuned itself automatically. The farm shone along with Peter and if he could have measured it, the Universe did too.

PRINTED AND BOUND BY:

Copytech (UK) Limited trading as Printondemand-worldwide,
9 Culley Court, Bakewell Road, Orton Southgate.
Peterborough, PE2 6XD, United Kingdom.